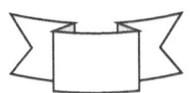

Chapter One

Near Miss

Saturday, May 17

The wave slapped the hull like a wrecking ball hitting a house.

"Wow! If I didn't know better, I'd bet that dude up on the wall just shot a cannon at us," Rachel Fuller said to her brother Adam, laughing. Rachel and Adam and Rachel were both hiked out of the cockpit in the sleek, sixty-five year old Kettenburg Pacific Class sailboat.

"That soldier couldn't be over fourteen years old!" Adam responded. Adam had observed from trips south of the border that

Méxican Army soldiers tended to the young side. He speculated they smoked cigarettes to add a few years to their appearance, not because they liked them.

Adam hauled in the main sheet, improving the mainsail's shape to gain speed. He was thinking life couldn't get any better as he watched Rachel trimming the jib. He smiled to himself as he saw her toss her head and run her fingers through her hair to smooth it out. That was trademark Rachel. His eyes teared up thinking about not sailing with her again after this summer. He'd miss her door slamming in the house, late night crime discussions and her stealing his treasures to trade for something she wanted from him.

Adam admired his sister's sailing outfit which included sunglasses with bands to hold them on, a red windbreaker jacket over blue tee shirt, white shorts and blue Topsiders, no socks. Adam wore his Halsey surfing shirt with a blue windbreaker and black shorts, and adjusted his red sailing cap to keep it firmly in place. Adam sailed barefoot even in colder weather. Rachel wisely left her sailing hat below in the cuddy to avoid losing it in the wind.

The wind was kicking up from the east. The normal wave fetch from the west was buffeted by the cross wind. More waves stood up and smacked the sailboat sending spray skyward and cascading back over the two sailors. Rachel screamed with delight.

A seal near the shore barked. The fog bank low over the water to the east and away from the islands was starting to dissipate. But the Baja California mainland eight miles to the east was still invisible.

"Remember when we snorkeled to the rocks over there and saw a crab the size of a dinner plate?" Rachel reminisced, pointing to the nearby shoreline of South Coronado.

Run for the Money
An Adventure in México

Copyright © 2016 by Bud Suiter

Suiter Publishing books may be ordered in electronic form through www.Scribd.com. *A Year in Andalucía!* is available for Kindle on Amazon. Many of the books are or will soon be available in paperback through Amazon.com and Amazon.co.uk. *Lost Art* is available in paperback by contacting the publisher at rumfunny@gmail.com.

Information about author Bud Suiter is found on the Suiter Publishing page on Facebook.

Due to the dynamic nature of the Internet, any web addresses or links may have changed since publication and may no longer be valid.

ISBN: 978-0-9853806-7-0

Printed by Create Space

Acknowledgements

I'd like to thank and recognize my own kids, Tom, Elizabeth and Katherine, who taught me more about teenage life than I learned when I was that age. Their careers in public relations, medicine, and book publishing should be an inspiration for every high schooler reading this. You can do it, too.

Special thanks to my wife Gaynor who encouraged me with her positive spirit to finish the Fuller series, this being the third of three novels. The first two are *Death by Design* and *Lost Art*. She provided insightful comments on the many revisions to the manuscripts and designed the cover of *Run for the Money.*

I want to thank my science students at *The Francis Parker School* in San Diego for the insights into the minds of high schoolers as well as their adventures which are found under disguise in *Run for the Money.* Any mistakes and exaggerations are, of course, mine.

My *Parker* colleagues contributed to the spirit of the Adam and Rachel Fuller series, especially: Dr. Lee Pierson, Head of School when I began writing the trilogy, who encouraged innovation in the classroom; Ms. Sharon Carroll, Head of Middle School, who instantly fulfilled support requests to achieve excellence in the mission; Mr. Patrick Mitchell, Head of Upper School, a steady hand at the tiller who took risks and tried new ideas; and the entire faculty, particularly the science teachers.

I relish the memories of working with this group of talented educators.

Photo and other credits: Cover adapted by Gaynor Coller-Suiter from Google Images: Teotihuacán feathered serpent god Quétzalcoatl representing the wind and the planet Venus. This ancient deity has been traced to the late first century BCE. At that time, Teotihuacán was one of the largest cities in the world with nearly two hundred thousand inhabitants. They used the feathered serpent as a political and religious symbol. This god later spread throughout Mesoamerica into the Mayan and Aztec cultures. The image captures the rich history and culture of México.

The descriptions of the art of the Teotihuacán and earlier Olmec civilizations are courtesy of the Metropolitan Museum of Art, Manhattan, New York, New York.

Other photos are from Google Images unless otherwise identified.

Bud Suiter, February 2016

"You bet. Still don't know what kind that was. Look at these little red crabs." They both saw the huge number of three inch long orange red crabs swimming by the boat near the surface. Adam thought it was unusual to see them this far north in such large numbers. He'd seen tons of them four hundred miles further south in Magdalena Bay. From sophomore year oceanography, Adam remembered that this red crab, *Pleuroncodes planipes,* is the most abundant species in the open sea. They're self-propelled creatures found on the east coast of the Pacific but mostly in the southern part of the California Current. Large swarms of these crabs can be several kilometers long, a feast for the lucky whale that chances upon them.

"Food chain for the blue whales," Rachel said as if reading Adam's thoughts.

"Two blues were spotted off the coast of San Diego last week. They usually show up further out. Krill's their favorite lunch." Blues, like all baleen whales, strain krill from the water in huge quantities. When they eat, they eat a lot.

Today, the pair was sailing *Seasalt* in Méxican waters sixteen miles south of San Diego near the Coronado Islands. The three islands were now all visible, showing off their spectacular soaring, rocky peaks devoid of trees and shrubs, basking in the sun.

A brown pelican dived into the water near their boat scoring a silvery fish about six inches long. Adam thought about the predominantly left handedness of pelicans. Young pelicans flying above the sea looking for fish turn their left eye to the target below the waves. After many dives and impacts with the water over the years cause that eye to go blind, pelicans become righties. When the right eye gives up, they can no longer fish and soon starve to death.

Adam focused his attention on the young Méxican Army soldier, now standing high above them behind a whitewashed stucco wall. He appeared to be looking down at *Seasalt*, carefully following the Fuller's progress south and clutching an AK-47 automatic assault rifle.

"What do you think that soldier is planning to do with us?" Rachel mused rhetorically, as they moved steadily away from the AK-47. Adam didn't respond, but he knew that trespassing started as soon as you set foot on the island. He also knew the islands were off limits to tourists and zealously guarded. Years earlier there had been a gambling casino in the building now occupied by the Méxican Army. Today the Army's goal was to protect the islands from human adventurers and maintain an offshore post to keep an eye on local coastal shipping and pleasure boat traffic. Especially those bringing illegal people or drugs north.

The Fullers left the dock at the San Diego Yacht Club around nine that morning with unusually good offshore winds brewing. With strong winds, they'd made the passage to the east side of South Coronado, the largest and furthest south of the three islands, in just three hours. They'd see the light colored sandy ocean bottom there under their boat that provides the best anchorage in thirty feet of water. Here the island shielded the anchorage from the normally prevailing westerly's. Today, the ocean was a steely grey, reflecting the remnants of the fog.

"Hey! I hear something!" Adam shouted, straining to see into the thinning fog bank between the islands and the mainland to the east. The sound of high powered, high RPM motors now competed with barking seals and cries of seagulls and cormorants. "It's a speedboat and it's moving fast."

Suddenly they both saw the bright red craft bearing down on them, a shark's mouth painted on the bow.

"Fall off!" Rachel shouted at Adam.

"When everything's coming your way, you're in the wrong lane," Adam shouted back as he pushed the tiller sharply away and the bow of the sailboat moved quickly off the speedboat's path. They could see a dark skinned, heavyset figure at the wheel of the speedboat wearing sunglasses, his black hair slicked back. His face bore no expression. There were pock marks visible on his face even at this distance.

The speedboat passed within feet of *Seasalt*, buffeting the Fullers in its wake, forcing a second course correction. "I hate it when speedboats do that! No respect!" Rachel shouted.

A second figure standing up in the speedboat with long blonde hair tied back in a pig tail shouted in Spanish at the Fullers, "Watch out! Next time we'll hit you and that won't be good for your pretty boat!"

"Rach, those men are sickos!"

"They're blaming *us*. Did you see the slash across the driver's chin?" Rachel screeched, now a quivering pillar of indignation.

"Must have caught the business end of a sharp knife," Adam continued the thought. "And that toad with the ponytail!"

"Adam, look!" Rachel shouted. The soldier, joined by two others, was pointing his machine gun at the speedboat now rapidly disappearing to the north. Suddenly, a loud burst of gunfire echoed off the rocky coast and bullets raked the water near the speedboat. The ponytailed companion in the speedboat raised a rifle and fired back at the soldiers, laughing as he did. One of the three soldiers shouted, ducked low, and ran back into the white bungalow just behind the wall.

A second soldier raised his AK-47 and began shooting. The firing continued from both sides, with two automatic guns now vying for a hit on the powerful red craft headed north. The man with the rifle in the speedboat responded and bullets caromed off the wall in front of the soldiers.

The Fullers sailed quickly away from the shooting. "That was incredible, Adam. Bet that speedboat is on their wanted list," said Rachel. "Those are the kind of boats you read about in the newspapers that run drugs up the coast."

"Rach, I hope the soldiers sink them. That's what they deserve."

Then Adam continued, "A Fountain speedboat like that one can do ninety knots across the water. No Coast Guard cutter would have a chance of catching them."

Rachel responded, "They need a helicopter."

"By the time a helicopter got here, they'd be long gone." As if to prove his words, the speedboat disappeared into the fog headed north. The twin 700 HP Mercury outboards were now muted and the roar diminished. But before two minutes had passed, the distinct 'whump, whump' of helicopter blades joined the cacophony of sounds in this normally quiet place.

"No sooner said than here they come," Adam said, flashing Rachel a grin. "This is going to be something!" The Méxican army helicopter passed directly over *Seasalt* which was knocked about with the wind from the blades. The chopper banked sharply right past the Army outpost and also headed north into the fog.

"Hey," Adam shouted over the noise, "that's one of their new

Blackhawk BH-60 helicopters. They're like two hundred miles an hour fast."

"I'd be amazed if they don't catch them now. Come on, helicopter!" Rachel was shouting over the noise. Minutes later the sound of the helicopter's fifty millimeter cannons could be heard in the distance, followed by a 'whooshing' that sounded to Adam like a rocket propelled grenade. Suddenly, there was an explosion. But the rapidly diminishing scream of the boat's twin outboards continued.

"Uh, oh," Adam said. "I don't hear the helicopter anymore." The hair on the back of his neck stood straight up at the thought.

Seasalt was now approaching the south end of South Coronado Island, the sudden silence without the helicopter like a deafening roar of its own. Even the ever-noisy gulls had momentarily quieted down.

"Let's get out of here, Rach. This is too much. Ready about!"

"Ready." Rachel responded, sounding much subdued.

"Helm's a lee!" Adam said. *Seasalt* responded to Adam pushing the tiller far over to the downwind side of the boat. She came around through the sharpening breeze onto the opposite tack, heading for home. Rachel re-cleated the jib sheet on the downwind side, the foresail snapping taut in the breeze. White caps formed on the surface of the water making sailing more challenging, promising a quick return trip. The sun now showed brilliantly. The fog was gone.

They could no longer see or hear the speedboat, either. Adam guessed it had gone outside Middle Coronado Island and was miles west of the Fuller's return course north to Pt. Loma.

Adam said, "That was a mess. Better not tell Mom and Dad.

They'll ground me for sure on going to México. I'd like to keep my summer job."

"I'm not sure I'd want to keep it, if I were you."

To lighten the mood, Adam said, "Hey, little sister, I'm going to miss these sailing trips with you." They'd made this journey to the Coronados several times a year the last few years but with Adam headed to college in the east these adventures were over.

"Yep," Rachel responded. "I'll have to bring a boyfriend from now on. You're finished, Adam. You'll have to trade in your sailing gear for ice skates at Dartmouth. The only water you'll see there is frozen."

"I'll be sailing at Dartmouth smarty pants but on Lake Mascoma instead of the Pacific Ocean, that's all. The ice will be gone by mid-April. That gives me thirty days on the water before I'm home again, so I'll take my sailing gear." Adam was smiling but he had a lump in his throat thinking about leaving Rachel and San Diego, a change that would lead to more changes. The results he knew would never again be the same.

The pair talked about the coming weekend, forgetting the red speedboat for the moment.

Then Rachel brought up the oceanography discussion again. She'd gone bonkers with the news about the black clouds hanging over the world's oceans. In fact, she told Adam now, she was thinking about switching her career goal from astronomy to marine biology.

"Dad's going to love that, Rach," he interjected. Mr. Fuller was currently chairman of the astronomy department at San Diego State University. Rachel found her Dad's research totally fascinating and had written science papers with astronomy flair, like her seventh grade *Terraforming Mars* report.

They sailed north enjoying the sun and the water for fifteen minutes without talking.

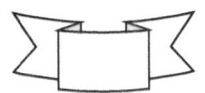

Chapter Two

Oceanography

Later, Same Day

Rachel broke the silence, turning to face aft from her starboard perch forward in the cockpit.

"Adam," Rachel opined, "if we don't fix our oceans now, they'll be dead by the time we send men to Mars. What would be the point of going to Mars if there are no fish, coral or whales left here?" Rachel was quite agitated, Adam could see, as she always was when confronted with injustice. In this case, environmental injustice.

A wave smacked *Seasalt* and the boat lurched.

Rachel went on about the oceans, while Adam tuned out, focused on the now deep blue water and watching for dolphins and whales. If Adam had paid attention to Rachel ranting on, he'd have heard about the cod fish diminishing in the Atlantic Ocean, the decline in the number of eight hundred pound green sea turtles, and the virtual disappearance of hammerhead sharks.

Adam glanced up at the rigging, strained by the forces of nature. He was amazed that the wooden mast was still standing after all these years. A family friend loaned them the thirty two foot long boat for the day. Despite her regular and often racing schedule, the varnished dark mahogany trim on her toe rail and in the cockpit gleamed like new in the early afternoon sun.

Adam heard the last remark about the hammerheads and responded, "Dad said he met the ant scientist, Edward O. Wilson, last year. Wilson says the Earth is already in its sixth major extinction event. This one is caused by us. But extinction is hard to believe with all the animals we saw today. They're everywhere." Adam, who knew better, was playing devil's advocate to keep Rachel stirred up.

"You're not even close, Adam," she snapped back. "Josh told me about the Warner School science lecture last week. Dr. Jeremy Jackson from Scripps spoke there about that very question." Warner is a private school about the size of Seaside. They compete for students, in sports and in college admissions rates. Scripps Institute of Oceanography is the renowned research center in La Jolla, CA.

"Are you still seeing Josh, Rach? I thought he was history after Dad blew up." Josh Billingsley and Rachel had been an item for a few months.

"We're just friends now. Wasn't his fault that he crashed his car and couldn't get me home until four in the morning. Drunk driver cut us off. We still talk on the phone." Josh, a Warner senior, had dated Rachel after she and Dave Rydell broke up in November.

Rachel continued. "Pay attention to the oceanography, Adam! Jackson showed that the number of big fish in the ocean is declining faster than ever. He showed a picture from a fishing tournament in Key West, Florida which compared the sizes of winning fish over the last twenty five years."

"What happened?" Adam asked, although he knew the answer.

"The winning fish have dropped from seven feet long to less than two feet in the same tournament at the same time of the year. In one case, even the same fishing boat was used all those years."

Adam said, "The big fish are getting smarter."

"Adam!" Rachel shrieked.

"Just kidding, Rach. I've seen photos of tournament winning bill fish caught off Cabo. Same story. They're shrinking, too." Cabo San Lucas is at the southern tip of the Baja California peninsula which stretches a thousand miles south of San Diego. Cabo is where the Pacific Ocean meets the Sea of Cortez.

The only sailing instrument in the sailboat, known as a 'PC' for Pacific Class, was a compass in the cockpit, but Adam could see Pt. Loma and knew they were on course due north without looking at the compass. In fog like they had earlier, the compass was the only hope for getting back.

Seasalt left Middle Coronado and North Coronado Islands behind. The wind held steady at seventeen knots from the east, the high pressure Santa Ana condition east of San Diego flexing its muscles.

Rachel glanced back at the three islands. Not a wisp of fog or cloud anywhere. She turned back to Adam and continued the arguments about the status of the ocean.

Rachel and Adam both liked the whales and dolphins best, the cetaceans. Rachel mentioned that the carnivorous gray whales eat two to four tons of krill, a Norwegian word meaning whale food, a day during the feeding season to survive the rest of the year. The whales come north in March for the summer primarily around the Channel Islands, Monterey Bay, the Farallon Islands and Cordell Bank west of San Francisco, and as far north as Alaska. During the winter months, they migrate to the warmer waters from México to Costa Rica for calving and adventure. Sailboats and powerboats follow the same pattern except their owners don't calve and the boaters return later than the whales.

So protecting krill is crucial for the long-term viability of other species that depend on krill for food. The highly nutritious nature of krill is precisely what makes it so important to the marine food web -- its rich omega-3 oils are vital for the dietary needs of whales, penguins and other marine predators. Many salmon farmers catch krill to feed their fish up to market size. This reduces the krill available in the wild.

In order to help protect the whale food supply, the National Oceanographic and Atmospheric Administration (NOAA) announced a ban on krill harvesting in a wide section of the Pacific Ocean off the coasts of Washington, Oregon and California in 2009. But krill are mostly taken off Antarctica, where scientists have raised concerns the fishing there has upset the food web.

But the big issues Rachel ripped into are the death of the world's coral reefs and the jellyfish explosion.

The pair argued about coral reefs dying due to increased acicity of ocean water from atmospheric carbon dioxide dissolving in the water.

"So what do we do about it?" Adam questioned.

Rachel reached into her boat bag and pulled out a jar of black powder. "I forgot. This is my contribution. Iron powder indirectly absorbs carbon dioxide dissolved in the water so I've decided to bring some every time I go sailing."

She explained that phytoplankton thrive on iron so iron fertilization creates phytoplankton blooms in the ocean. Phytoplankton breathe in carbon dioxide which has been absorbed into the ocean from the atmosphere. These phytoplankton are not relying on the nutrients from fertilizer so continue to survive after the bloom. The carbon dioxide is reduced by the phytoplankton and less ends up as carbonic acid in the ocean. Less carbonic acid in the water means fewer calcium carbonate shells on reef organisms are dissolved by the acid, a process which kills the animals in the shells.

The reefs thrive with less carbonic acid. Rachel said she bet that if everybody who went out for a day sail brought a pound of iron powder and dumped it in the water, this nasty trend would be reversed.

Adam said, "Rach, great idea, but let's test the math. I've heard there are five hundred thousand federally documented recreational boats and probably that many more state documented boats in U.S. waters. So call it a million boats. If each boat went out twelve times a year and dropped one pound of iron powder, we're talking twelve million pounds a year. That's just the U.S., but that's just a drop in the ocean, too."

"Adam, we've got to start somewhere. And you're right we'd have to drop twelve million tons a year, not pounds, to make any real difference."

Then Rachel switched to the dead zones in the oceans as the siblings were already better than halfway to Point Loma. The dead zones are areas of low oxygen where the only things that survive are jellyfish.

"Yeah," Adam interjected as they passed a lobster pot marker floating on the surface, "remember those black jellyfish floating around San Diego Bay last year? They were everywhere and maybe fourteen inches in diameter."

"May have shown up as a result of the dead zone off La Jolla a few years back," Rachel said.

Dead zones are caused by fertilizer and sewage runoff into the ocean which also causes a bloom of phytoplankton, but for different reasons. The nitrogen and phosphorus from the fertilizer are soon used up, so without food, the phytoplankton die. Oxygen is sucked out of the water as the dead plankton rot. The dead zone that results in the Gulf of México is as big as the state of New Jersey. Rachel said that worldwide there were now over four hundred dead zones, some bigger than the one in the Gulf.

Rachel continued, "But let me answer the question Mr. Volpini raises about how big this job of saving the oceans is. The problems are social, political and economic. So we each do everything we can do!" Rachel was now shouting into the wind. Adam thought that was symbolic when you considered the magnitude of the problem and her proposed solution.

They were both quiet awhile as they approached the tip of Pt. Loma. Boat traffic picked up, forcing Adam to focus outside the boat.

Then Rachel spoke again. "Mr. V is taking our oceanography class out on a Scripps research ship. We'll do carbon dioxide absorption experiments." The Scripps Institute operates four research vessels including the ship they'd take, the *Roger Revelle*, plus the research platform, FLIP, which the pair passed on the left as they sailed around the northwest end of Shelter Island. The *Roger Revelle*, built in 1996, is two hundred seventy seven feet long. Scripps takes guests on research trips.

"That's cool. We didn't get to do that. Volpini just gets better with age," Adam said. "What's the experiment?"

"We're putting a ton of iron dust into the ocean. We'll be out sixty miles to avoid the long shore currents in close. The scientists will measure the density of plankton and acidity of the water over the following thirty days to see what happens. We'll be out for the first two days of the experiment. I can't wait."

"Seems like a tiny experiment when you consider the size of the ocean," Adam remarked, shaking his head.

"Sure, but if it works the way we think it will, then much larger scale projects can be funded by the countries of the world to do the rest of the job."

Rachel had to point out another sore spot for scientists trying to save the oceans: sewage treatment. San Diego municipal sewage treatment was primary only. San Diego applies for and gets waivers on the Federal requirement to upgrade from primary to tertiary treatment. Primary treatment takes out solid matter and tertiary even gets most of the bacteria out. But the billions of dollars required for the upgrade were just not available. In México, even primary treatment was not universal. Raw sewage from Tijuana is dumped straight into the ocean. The growing pharmaceutical drug content of sewage was now a source of alarm.

Rachel wrapped up the discussion by saying, "We can also set up very large Marine Protected Areas, like the one up in the Channel Islands, ban persistent pesticides and pharmaceuticals, and push for green energy and more efficient cars. There's plenty we can do."

They passed the many yacht clubs and marinas on Shelter Island, docking at four 4 PM. After washing the white hulled boat down with a hose and toweling off the varnished bright work to eliminate water spots, the pair secured the blue boat covers. Then Adam turned to Rachel and putting his finger to his lips said, "Mum's the word, Rach, about what happened today. I want that job in Ensenada."

Rachel looked at Adam but said nothing as the pair walked quickly up the dock ramp and disappeared into the parking lot.

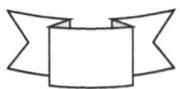

Chapter Three

The Mountains

Sunday, May 18

Next morning, Mr. Fuller rousted Adam out of bed at 6:30 A.M. For Adam, this was an ungodly hour considering Adam hadn't gotten to bed until 2 AM after his movie date with Julie Sanders.

"Let's beat the rush up the mountain, Adam," he said. An early morning breakfast in the mountains was a Fuller family tradition. With Adam soon off to college there wouldn't be many more of these. Just the two of them would go today.

"DAD!" Adam moaned as he always did this early in the morning. But Adam got up anyway, took a quick shower and got dressed.

Adam combed his hair, looking into the bathroom mirror. Suddenly, for no apparent reason, he recalled the day his mother had discovered two *Playboy* magazines under his bed. His face flushed at the thought. She hadn't been mad that he had them but rather that he was hiding them. Adam had a tendency to hide things from his parents. You can't tell your parents everything, he mused to himself. It's just too embarrassing.

And what was that on his chin? Another pimple? Where do they come from? Julie probably saw this one starting last night. Is there a hidden pimple barrel ready to supply new pimples as soon as you get a date?

Adam grabbed his Seaside High School sailing jacket and went out to the living room. Mr. Fuller was ready to go.

Outside the Fuller garage, the blue-purple jacaranda trees were in full bloom as were the blue agapanthus. Adam popped the garage door. They jumped into his Dad's beloved Jaguar XK E roadster and headed east on Interstate 8. Roger Fuller bought the car new and all these years later it still looked just like it came off the showroom floor. Adam loved driving the Jag when he could convince his Dad to let him but today Mr. Fuller had the wheel.

Fuller Jaguar XK E with covered headlamps, legal for new cars until 1968

"Dad, what've you and Mom decided about Rachel going to the U2 concert with Mike Nelson?" Mike was the 6'4" dark haired, bushy browed hunk Rachel was now excited about.

"We'll talk about that tonight with your mother and Rachel."

Adam pressed on anyway. "I think you should let Rachel go. Mike aced his driver's test and he's a good guy, not crazy or like that." Mike Nelson had a crush on Rachel, which Adam knew because Mike had so confided to Adam. But Rachel really warmed up to Mike when he asked her to go with him to see her favorite music group.

"I thought you'd come to Rachel's rescue," Mr. Fuller said. Adam had gone through the same issues about driving alone with a date in a car when he'd gotten his license a year earlier. The pain of those arguments still lingered. "Let's save this discussion for tonight."

The six thousand foot high Laguna Mountains hid the rising sun.

Adam was glad he had a windbreaker on. Traffic was negligible at this hour. The quiet purr of the Jaguar's six cylinder motor was reassuring as they climbed to four thousand feet. They arrived at Route 79 then headed north on the winding, narrow and challenging road.

Mr. Fuller kept the car in the lower gears using the power band of the engine to maximum effect. Adam knew this 1948 twin cam motor design was used in the 1950's Jaguar race cars which won the French Le Mans 24 Hour motor race five times. Disk brakes now standard on most modern day production sedans were pioneered by Jaguar at Le Mans in 1953. Mr. Fuller used the brakes hard to slow for the hairpin bends, the slowest of which he took in first gear. They didn't talk much as they savored the drive under the canopy of green live oak trees, their branches spread over the road. At one point, they saw five wild turkeys scratching for food in the deep spring grass.

"Remember the time we saw the bobcat over there?" Adam said, pointing up the hill to the left.

"You bet. We've seen a few coyotes around here, too," his Dad responded.

Morning mists rose off the wet grey-green meadows. Mr. Fuller commented, "Adam, those mists remind me of John Watt." John Watt was one of Mr. Fuller's astronomy Ph.D. candidates at SDSU. His Dad liked to tell stories about John.

Adam sighed, "OK, Dad, what's John up to now."

"Friday he showed me his latest research on Neptune's misty methane atmosphere. He's convinced that with the high temperature and pressure there, real diamonds will precipitate instead of hailstones like we get here on Earth. He's concluded that Neptune has a diamond cycle instead of a water cycle."

Adam said, "Tight! Rachel would be on fire for that." Mr. Fuller chuckled at the thought and glanced over at Adam.

Adam continued, "Nice if John could bring those diamonds back from Neptune to pay for his PhD." Adam paused then said, "But the astronomy theory I like best is that the rings of Saturn are made of lost airline luggage."

"Good one, Adam. I've used that in my freshman astronomy course," Mr. Fuller said, laughing. They were having fun on boy's day out.

The Fullers pulled into the Cuyamaca Restaurant parking lot, went in and took a window seat overlooking the lake. A little piece of Austria in the southern California mountains. The cuckoo clock on the wall chimed 8 AM.

Glancing around the almost empty restaurant, Adam observed the aged knotted pine board walls decorated with three deer heads, each sporting a large rack of antlers. The windows looking out on the lake were framed with red Cranbrook curtains. Outside, the sun glistened off the deep blue water of Lake Cuyamaca, and thin white clouds dotted the sky. Adam reflected that in winter the clouds might be dark gray and right down on the water, obscuring the far shores of the lake.

An attractive blonde haired waitress appeared wearing a white apron. "Good morning, men, what will it be today?"

"Beer for both of us, Judy!" Mr. Fuller joked.

"And who would be driving today, Professor?" she shot back. The Fullers were well known here and Mr. Fuller's humor appreciated. Judy knew that Adam was not old enough for beer.

Mr. Fuller and Adam both ordered the breakfast special: Austrian sausage, fried eggs sunny side, sourdough toast, applesauce and juice. Mr. Fuller also ordered his usual eye-opener, Austrian Edelweiss wheat beer. The breakfasts were quickly served.

Adam read the label on the Edelweiss bottle: "Seit 1475". A relative newcomer, Adam thought to himself. The Spåten brewery in Germany had been going since 1397, nearly one hundred years earlier. There was usually a six pack of Spåten in the fridge at home, his Dad's favorite.

Aloud, Adam said, "Beer companies are survivors."

"Beer's a good business. It self sustains." Mr. Fuller responded. Then he continued as Adam attacked his breakfast, "We're going to hit the fund raising targets for the new hundred inch telescope this summer which means we'll start construction before you leave for college. This bigger telescope will boost the research programs."

"You've sure spent a bunch of time over the last two years with potential donors, Dad. We didn't see much of you there for a while."

"Should be worth it, Adam. This move keeps SDSU in the forefront of space research. My career's at stake here." Adam smiled. Mr. Fuller liked to over-dramatize.

"SDSU's work on charge coupled device cameras should help you keep your job, Dad."

"You had a top notch opportunity there last summer working on those cameras."

Adam said "You bet! No pay but I learned a ton. One of the cameras I worked on was sold to the University of Texas."

"Our cameras replace film cameras in astronomy because they capture seventy five percent of the incoming light while film records five percent. In fact, the big film companies are no longer in the film business because the same thing has happened with consumer cameras using different technology."

"Guess technology companies are risky bets," Adam responded. "But SDSU has another advantage, Dad. Their Mt.

Laguna astronomy facilities are a hundred feet higher than Mt. Palomar." At Mt. Palomar the world's largest telescope from 1948 to 1990 is sited and still operating north of the Cuyamaca Restaurant and not far from the SDSU telescopes.

"A hundred feet counts, Adam." Then turning in his seat, Mr. Fuller exclaimed, "Hey, buddy!" His friend Steve Fletcher was sitting down at the next table. Steve's granddad, Colonel Ed Fletcher, had written a book about the history of San Diego, including some good stories about the nearby abandoned gold mines and the Kumayaay and Cuyamaca Indian tribes which had called these mountains home for centuries.

"Adam, you got your bags packed for Dartmouth yet?" Steve said, smiling.

Before Adam could respond, the sound of a glass crashing to the floor caused Adam to look to his left.

Adam saw a man jump up from the table closest to the kitchen and shout at Judy.

"How can you be so clumsy!" He screamed in heavily accented, growly English. Judy had been carrying a water glass balanced on a tray. Water splashed onto the screamer's pants before the glass fell to the floor, breaking into a million sparkling pieces. Judy, distraught, was apologizing when the man turned toward Adam. Adam froze.

"Dad," Adam whispered under his breath. "That man almost hit us off South Coronado yesterday with his speed boat. Look at his face!" Mr. Fuller turned and noted the dark hair and skin and the chin scar. Adam omitted telling about the gunfight with the helicopter.

"Wow, must have been a nasty fight. What a scar! He's one angry hombre," Mr. Fuller said.

"Scarface!" Adam quietly exclaimed to Mr. Fuller.

Scarface had a breakfast companion who rose from the table and quickly left the restaurant. The companion's red jacket was emblazoned on the back with a gold "Eagles" logo, identified with nearby Mountain High School.

The chirp of tires on pavement rang through the restaurant, announcing the rapid departure of Scarface's friend. The heavyset man threw down a large bill on the table, and stormed out, too, forgetting that accounts are squared up at the cashier by the front door.

A throaty sounding V-8 engined-car started in the parking lot outside. Adam rose and moved quickly to the front of the restaurant and looked out.

He saw a new black BMW 545 with dark tinted windows move quickly in reverse, bumping the Fuller's car which was parked beside it. With a screech from the oversized, low profile tires, the car headed south on Route 79. Adam saw part of the license plate as the car disappeared. The number, obscured by the glint of sunlight on the plastic cover over the plate, was Frontera BC "291XR..." A Baja California, México, license plate! Adam pulled out his cell phone and made note of the number. Plastic covers over license plates were now illegal in the State of California, Adam thought, but apparently not in Baja.

Upset, Adam ran outside, and noticed the glint of sunlight off a white powder on the pavement. On a hunch, he leaned down and took a plastic Ziploc bag out of his pocket. With his Swiss Army knife, he scraped as much of the powder into the bag as he could.

When Mr. Fuller arrived in the parking lot, Adam was standing, looking down the road.

"Dad, that guy bumped our car and didn't stop!"

Mr. Fuller said, "Did you get the license number?"

"I got part of it." Adam had an idea he wanted to pursue before telling his Dad about the powder.

Mr. Fuller continued, "Let's finish breakfast. Whatever damage he caused looks minor. We'll check it again before we leave."

They returned to the table. Judy came over, and said, "Professor Fuller, that man was really upset. I feel bad for spilling water on him. His friend had his foot out in the aisle and I didn't see it."

"Judy, something else was bothering that guy - the water just pushed him over the edge," Mr. Fuller responded.

"How are you two doing here? Refills on coffee?" Judy had quickly regained her composure.

"Thanks. Coffee would be great. Adam, apple strudel?"

"You bet!" Adam said.

"Adam, tell me what happened yesterday." Adam recounted the sailing adventure he and Rachel had had, his blue eyes flashing when he described the near miss with the speed boat. But Adam didn't reveal all.

"I can't believe I see this guy twice in two days!" Adam concluded, indignant.

"You know what they say, Adam, things happen in three's. You may see him again, so be prepared."

Adam didn't think this was very funny. "Yeah, right Dad. Sure hope not."

"Let's stop in Julian for an apple pie. You drive on the way home, Adam."

While Mr. Fuller paid the bill, Adam went outside to the car. He scraped the black paint left by the BMW on a spot below their car's left rear bumper into a second plastic bag. That he tucked into his pocket, too. The damage had been minimal. When Mr. Fuller emerged from the restaurant again, Adam had the car running, a big grin on his face.

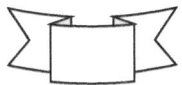

Chapter Four

The Lab

Early Monday, May 19

Adam and Rachel arrived at the lab a few minutes before 7 AM Monday morning.   Adam set this up with a phone call to Mr. Volpini late Sunday.   Mr. V was already at work and ready for testing the mystery powder.

"Your lab never changes, Mr. Volpini," Adam said by way of combining a greeting and a compliment. "Always neat and clean and promising."

Rachel chimed in. "Bet you're doing organic chemistry, Mr. V. I can tell by the smell of fruit. Esters. I loved building those saturated and unsaturated hydrocarbon models."

"Thanks guys, I appreciate that. These labs take a lot of time to prepare and clean up and it's nice to know someone enjoys it," Mr. V said. Then, turning to Adam, Volpini barked, "But whaddya mean, nothing has changed? Look! I've got a new portable PC to drive the telescope." Adam looked and winced at having missed it.

"Way cool. How does it work?" Rachel said.

"You let the scope align itself while you drink coffee. Then you select the object from the PC screen you want to see. The PC moves the scope and aligns to the object for you. See maybe a hundred sky objects a night instead of fifteen. Even has a microphone option so you can control the telescope by voice commands. And the telescope talks back to you."

"I didn't know PC's spoke Italian, Mr. V," Adam quipped.

Volpini grinned at Adam's joke and said, "Italian's the highest form of English, Adam. But OK you two, let's get to work. Here's the powder." Glancing at a reference book on his table, Mr. V continued, "I'm going to guess that we have cocaine based on the appearance of the powder. Let's test this hypothesis."

Mr. Volpini poured fifty milliliters of Clorox bleach into a two hundred milliliter graduated cylinder.

"What're you doing with the bleach?" Adam queried.

"Hold still squirt and keep your eyes peeled," Volpini shot back. "And remember your goggles." Adam was amazed that once again, Mr. Volpini had to remind him to put on his goggles. Some things don't change. Adam and Rachel put on their goggles.

"We really don't know what we're getting into here. Always protect your eyes first. Here, Rachel, take a spatula and put some of Adam's powder on the spatula. And Adam, put enough bleach from the graduated cylinder into this test tube to fill it about three quarters full."

When Rachel had the powder on the spatula, Volpini said, "Now, tap the powder from the spatula into the test tube and watch carefully what happens." Rachel proceeded noting that the powder looked more like finely granulated white sugar. She then exclaimed, "Wow, the powder makes a milky trail down into the clear bleach as it sinks."

"Team Fuller, your test just proved the hypothesis: we have cocaine. Your sample passed with flying colors. Let's get the rest of this powder down town to the police lab now." Mr. Volpini started locking up the room, and said, "I'll clean up the mess later. We can get down town and back before my first class today. How is your schedule?"

Adam said, "Fine, no classes today. I'm cleaning out my locker. AP's are over."

Rachel said, "I'm going to cut my first period class to join you. I don't want to miss this! That is, if you'll give me a pass."

"Let me think about the pass. Got the Ziploc bag?" Volpini said as he locked the door.

In the car on the way to the police crime lab, Mr. Volpini said, "Did you notice anything falling to the bottom of the test tube ahead of the milky white trails? If you had, you would have seen sugar, baking soda or another chemical in crystalline form used for cutting the cocaine. That stretches the amount available to sell and increases street profits. But if you're a buyer and think you're getting pure cocaine, you'll be a little upset to find that fifty or seventy five percent of what you paid for is just sugar. People get shot for trying to pass off cut cocaine as pure when it isn't."

Mr. Volpini continued, "There's another test to identify how much a sample has been cut from the pure cocaine. Drop the powder into alcohol which dissolves the cocaine, but not the sugar. The sugar falls to the bottom, you strain the sugar out, mass it on a balance beam, and compare that with the mass of the powder before you start. Pronto! You get the percentage that the drug has been cut."

"What does cocaine cost? I've heard you make big bucks on good stuff." Adam asked the question like he knew the answer.

"Goes for $2/gram in the mountains of Columbia but by the time it gets to San Diego, it can be $40 to $80/gram or more, depending on purity and who's selling it. And sellers usually don't know if the stuff is cut or won't tell if they do."

"And it all comes from Columbia, right?" Adam continued the questioning.

"Used to. The DEA has been working with the Columbian police and army so Columbian production is way down over the last ten years. Now more comes from Peru and Bolivia. There's less cooperation there with our government. It's like the 'whack a mole' game at the Del Mar Fair."

The trio pulled into the downtown police station where the crime lab operated. Jake Steinberg, Mr. V's buddy, met them at the front desk.

"Volpini, how come you're not in jail yet?" Jake greeted them.

"You guys just aren't fast enough to catch me, obviously. Jake, you know Rachel and Adam Fuller."

"You bet. Good to see you again." Rachel and Adam both shook Steinberg's hand.

Volpini continued, "Adam found some powder in the mountains yesterday and I told him he needs to talk with you. We tested the powder this morning and it's cocaine. Adam, give the man the envelope so we don't get arrested here. Jake seems to think I ought to be in jail anyway."

Steinberg took the envelope with the Ziploc bag inside. He turned to Rachel and asked if she knew how heroin was produced, a question she didn't expect. She said she had a vague idea but she'd been focused on figuring out the cocaine thingy. So Steinberg explained that poppies are grown and harvested and processed to opium, which was then changed into morphine and finally to heroin. Afghanistan now supplies the world with opium, he confided, although a hundred and fifty years ago it all came from China. Now much of the black tar and brown heroin consumed in the U.S. is actually grown and distributed by the Méxican cartels.

With that gem hanging in the air, Steinberg and the bag of cocaine disappeared behind the formidable looking gray steel door. He reappeared a few minutes later, and said, "I think we need to take a statement, Adam. Would you mind talking to one of the detectives in the narcotics division?"

"You bet! Rachel, you stay here with Mr. Volpini." Adam disappeared behind the gray door.

"Rachel, it seemed to me that there was tension between you and Mike at the party last night." Mr. Volpini kept an eye out for his students.

"Mr. Volpini, my parents are being real jerks about letting me go to the U2 concert in Los Angeles next Saturday. Mike asked me to be his date, but I've put off accepting because my parents don't want me to drive with Mike. Can you believe it? What can I do?"

Volpini realized how stressful this was for Rachel. "Tell you what. I've been looking for two tickets to that concert myself. Dan Kuipol, my buddy in the athletic department, told me yesterday he wouldn't be able to use his tickets. What if I drove you and Mike up with Katie and me?"

Rachel quickly realized how many advantages there would be to sitting in the back seat of a car with Mike over two hours each way and Mr. Volpini driving. This is the solution!

"Mr. Volpini, thank you SO much. I'll see Mike today and make sure this works for him. He wanted to drive."

"Just tell him the gas and parking are on me. That should swing the deal. But I don't have the tickets yet. Dan may have sold them. I'll let you know."

Adam walked out the gray door.

"Wow, I never had so many questions. You'd think this was a really big deal," Adam said.

"Actually, it's a big deal. The only way drugs coming into this country can be stopped is if every bit of evidence is gathered, on every incident, every day. You're now part of the solution and you may not even go to jail over the head of it," Volpini said, a twinkle in his eye.

Jake Steinberg came out again, and said, "OK, Tony, our lab is verifying your work. Our test for cocaine is the same one you used, so I don't expect a different result. And we have Adam's statement." He turned to the science sleuths. "How did your interview with Detective Denton go, Adam?"

"He sure asked a lot of questions. I feel like I didn't see everything I should have, or maybe I should have taken notes to help me remember better."

"That's the nature of police questioning, Adam. The more we know, the better we do," Steinberg said. "Now, Rachel, for the rest of the story. Heroin as I mentioned comes from a certain poppy seed sap. Cocaine, on the other hand – which is likely what Adam found - comes from coca leaves. So both are plant based. Nature's way of providing natural relaxants and stimulants, I guess."

"Please continue," Rachel said.

"But we humans don't stop at what nature provides. In cocaine's case, we concentrate and change the chemical formula of what's in the leaf to get a more powerful stimulant. The first step, making coca paste, is a little like the first step in making wine from grapes in the old days. For coca paste, the leaves are stripped from the branches and put in a plastic vat. Men get in the vat and walk on the leaves in their bare feet. This process eventually produces coca paste when dried which is added to cigars and smoked. More zip than chewing leaves, but still mild and not very dangerous.

"Manufacturing a more concentrated form of cocaine to raise the narcotic effect requires adding chemicals to the paste. The result is cocaine hydrochloride, the white crystalline powder Adam found. This is snorted up the nose and the result is a higher thrill and kill factor.

Further processing cocaine hydrochloride gets you the highest coca-based mood elevator called free base or crack cocaine. That stuff is smoked and is much more dangerous to the user. Of course, cocaine is grown and synthesized in South America and distributed here through the Méxican cartels. End of lesson."

Mr. V. said, "Jake, thanks for the lesson and for taking over Adam's sample and for not putting me in jail. I owe you. We gotta head back to school". The trio left the crime lab and drove back to Seaside the way they came.

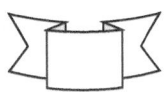

Chapter Five

Tijuana, México

Monday Afternoon, May 19

The bars on Calle Revolución in Tijuana were crowded by 3 PM on this weekday. Under-twenty-one party-hards from the States made this street their first stop for drinking and dancing. For a flat fee in some of the bars, you could drink as much as you wanted and stay as long as you wanted. More than one Americano left unable to walk in a straight line or maybe even walk at all. Some crawled away.

In the back room at Dos Hombres, one of the many bars, three men sat sipping Cazadores tequila. Cazadores is expensive tequila without the after effects of the low priced brands. A jukebox in the main part of the bar blared popular Méxican ballads which could be heard through the walls of the room.

The man whose presence dominated the room was Arturo Acevedo, the boss of a Tijuana drug cartel. He appeared to be a calm man who understood the ways of the world. His eyelids drooped in a way to make his eyes appear nearly closed as he surveyed the scene. Full lips were pursed to give his round, forty year old face a thoughtful look. He dressed the part of one in charge: an expensive looking gray suit with a dark red handkerchief folded in the left breast pocket, an open necked long sleeve white shirt with a gold necklace at his collar. He wore two gold rings on the fingers of his left hand and one ring on the right hand. Arturo looked at his scar faced companion who was dressed in black and thought to himself, 'Marcelo is one ugly, surly meat hook of a man. Bulging frog eyes on a scarred face. What a disaster. But totally loyal. I can live with his appearance because I own his loyalty.' Arturo cleared his throat.

"Marcelo, tell me about the helicopter."

"There's not much to report, Mr. Acevedo. Helicopter chased us on the way north. Manuelito put an RPG into it. Boom!"

Acevedo nodded appreciatively toward Manuelito. "And were you following our plan when this interruption occurred?"

"Yes sir, Mr. Acevedo. We were timing the outside run to Del Mar for a drug drop on the beach. If anyone'd stopped us, we were clean. But the opportunity to end the harassment from those idiots was there so we took it." Acevedo was still not smiling.

Then Acevedo said, "No worries, gentlemen. We have a high

level friend in the army who has filed his report saying the helicopter exploded from a gasoline leak. The army witnesses on the island have been compensated and will not discuss the matter. The U.S. government will never be aware that this incident took place in Méxican waters."

Acevedo paused for effect then said, "What next?"

Marcelo spoke again. "We continued the trip, timed the arrival off Del Mar and put our boat under cover in the lagoon to the north of the drop point. Under canvas so you can't see it from the air or the water. We hit the time objective. Our contact picked us up at the lagoon and drove us back across the border. Oscar will pick up the boat tonight and bring it back. The new boat is great. Really moves."

"Marcelo, next time don't tempt the Army by cutting close to the east side of the islands. Go further south and to the west of the islands. Keep the RPMs up a little higher to make up for the longer distance. Otherwise, good report. Now Marcelo, did you make the drop in Julian today?"

The man with the brutal scar on his chin nodded, but there was tension in his voice as he said, "I had to give our gringo friend credit again. Always more credit. He makes me angry. But he said he will pay us in full in two weeks. I charged him twenty percent for the extra time. Is this OK, Mr. Acevedo?"

Marcelo thought that Arturo Acevedo would agree, especially with the interest charge, but you never knew for sure what the big man wanted.

"Of course, Marcelo. We're bankers and reasonable men. We don't need the cash now anyway. But when you get the cash, be careful. The inspectors at the border have eyes." Acevedo could tell that Marcelo was agitated about the missed collection and didn't want to upset his lieutenant further.

"We always bring the cash across when Jaime is on duty. Just in case." Marcelo winked at Acevedo.

Acevedo now turned to the third man, who had a large tattoo on each of his biceps, the word "AMOR" written over the image of a skull and crossbones. He was well over six feet tall and obviously strong. Acevedo had known Manuelito since they both were five years old growing up together on the barrio streets. He knew that Manuelito had no morals whatsoever. The name Manuelito was the diminutive of Manuel and a term of affection coined by Acevedo. Acevedo knew that the scientific community would call him a sociopath. Manuelito would do anything he asked him to do. Manuelito, the second half of what he liked to call his M & Ms.

"Manuelito, if Marcelo's gringo friend, what's his name, Vincent, forgets to pay in June, arrange an accident or two. Let's say, a few broken windows, perhaps a dead dog with a note attached?"

Manuelito tossed off the remainder of his tequila, pushed his chair back and stood up. His blonde hair was pulled back in a ponytail that hung nearly a foot down his back. The bleach job on his hair was uneven if you looked too closely. He flexed his well-muscled arms and showed his tattoos to full effect.

"Mr. Acevedo, you know I'd do this before dark tonight if you wanted me to."

"I know you could, Manuelito. But I have bigger plans for tonight. The Rodriquez brothers in Ensenada are interested in a piece of our Tijuana business. I want to send them a message: you don't mess with the Acevedo family. Tomy Rodriquez will be at a fiesta in the San Nícolas Hotel in Ensenada tonight. He always uses valet parking. Bribe the valet. Take Tomy's fancy car for a little spin and see that it has a very bright ending, say off a cliff on the San Quintín road." The treacherous drops to the valley floor on the Ensenada to San Quintín road were scene to many such 'accidents.' Even real ones.

"With pleasure, Mr. Acevedo!" Manuelito said as he headed for the door. He paused, looking back at Arturo, his childhood friend, now one savvy businessman. For Manuelito, this car assignment should be fun. The music from the bar became noticeably louder as Manuelito opened the door. "I'll start now. There are a lot of turistas on the road. I want to have time to get ready. Shall I call the secret number and leave a message when I'm done?"

"Yes, Manuelito. And Manuelito, close the door."

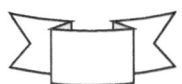

Chapter Six
México City
Wednesday, May 21

"México doesn't rain but it pours!" Mrs. Fuller explained to the family over breakfast. "Adam gets a job in México this summer and the México Tourism Board awards us a free trip to México City, all expenses paid."

She went on to state, in her polished travel agent manner, that despite the massive recession and the safety issues in México, the Board is reaching out to American tourists, even as new hotels are being built and México tourism from South America and Eastern

Europe is increasing. Finally she explained that she and Georgia Snitterbank, her assistant at the *Great Escape* travel agency, would be taking full advantage of México's kind offer by bringing Adam and Rachel along, too. The group would leave Friday and return Monday.

"Sounds fabulous and wish I could join you, but there's just too much going on here," Mr. Fuller interjected. "Adam's finished his classes. No issue there. I talked with Montenegro and he thinks a trip like this will give Adam more insight into the culture of México than he can get in Ensenada." He winked at Adam.

Mrs. Fuller said, taking the conversation back, "Your father can't go. But I talked to the head of Upper School and he agrees Rachel should join us. Christina Montenegro will be going, too." Adam visibly perked up at this news. A trip to México City with a Playmate of the Year! Culture is one thing but traveling with Christina in the entourage is promising.

Mrs. Fuller continued, "México is a modern agricultural state, especially in Baja, California. But México is also about history, art and ancient civilizations. We'll be staying at the Crowne Plaza Hotel not too far from the Zona Rosa."

"I remember seeing photographs of Chapúltepec Park," Rachel said. "Any chance we can go there, too?"

"The Tourism Board is taking us to the Teotihuacán pyramids on Saturday afternoon and to Chapúltepec Park on Sunday."

"Isn't there a history museum at Chapúltepec?" Rachel asked.

Mr. Fuller said, "Sure is. Museum of Cultural Anthropology, one of the best in the world."

Rachel was now smiling. But Adam's hope was that his mother would get behind him working in México once she got her batteries charged by the Tourism Board.

That Friday morning the travelers assembled at Tijuana International Airport in time to catch the 9 AM flight to México City. AeroMéxico was right on time. Their Boeing 737 was nearly new and Adam noted that the stewardesses were very pretty, with dark skin, jet black hair and teeth so white Tony Curtis would be put to shame. The one hour flight was unremarkable except for Rachel using her hands to block Adam's attempts to see more of Christina Montenegro seated just ahead of them and across the aisle. As they approached México City, the day was so clear that Mrs. Fuller could point out the pyramids northeast of the city.

"We'll be checking those out. Get a good look!" she said to Rachel and Adam. The pyramids were huge, Adam could see. The Pyramid of the Sun visually overpowered the Pyramid of the Moon to the north due to its immense size, and both were larger than the Quétzalcoatl Pyramid. "They were built two thousand years ago," she continued. "The city of Teotihuacán was the biggest in the world at the time. The pyramids were the centerpiece."

Georgia brought everyone back to the present by saying, "México City is known as the mile high city because it's located on a mile high plateau stretching flat in all directions. Harder to breathe at that altitude. Cars make it worse." She finished explaining that México City is planning rail transport to reduce air pollution in the future, that there used to be a large lake located where the city now stands which has been drained over the centuries. Earthquakes cause trouble because the dry lake bed just isn't stable.

Mrs. Fuller said, "Buildings take huge hits when the ground moves. Over twenty million people now live in the city which extends far beyond the original lake."

They quickly passed through the airport since the flight from Tijuana was a domestic one. They'd gone through the customs hassle before getting on the plane. Outside the airport, luggage was tossed into two taxis and the group was checked into the hotel forty minutes later. On the way in to the city, Mrs. Montenegro pointed out that her first trip to their hotel in 1986 when she was a little girl had been less than a year after the immense 1985 earthquake that leveled much of the city and killed over 10,000 people. She said that there'd been a giant crack down the front of the hotel then which was closed for repairs. No crack was in evidence now.

For the afternoon, Mrs. Fuller and Georgia Snitterbank planned to attend the opening of the travel agent convention which was being held at another hotel. So Adam and Rachel would be going shopping with Mrs. Montenegro in the Zona Rosa in the center of the city.

In the taxi again, Mrs. Montenegro sat between Rachel and Adam in the back seat and said, "You won't believe the shops here. Better than those in many European cities."

Adam asked, "So how did you meet Mr. Montenegro?" The taxi moved swiftly through traffic on the wide boulevard, dodging slower moving vehicles and trucks. The road was so wide here that cars stopping to drop off passengers barely slowed continuing traffic.

"I was on a promotional tour as Playmate of the Year. One of our stops was in San Diego. We had a short program at the Cox Arena at San Diego State. I tripped and almost fell as I stepped up on the stage. An arm reached out and rescued me. The arm was attached to Mr. Montenegro, a student usher for the event. Instant attraction! After the presentation he slipped his Méxican-American business card into my hand. His Dad started the trucking business, as you know, and

Ricardo was already working there part time. I wrote to him a week or so later. We had our first date within a month."

Rachel asked, "Where were you living then?"

"I was a freshman at the University of Chicago living in the dorms. I'd entered the contest for Playmate on a bet. Never thought I'd become a bunny or be elected Playmate of the Year. When I made it I was able to continue my studies and graduate on time. So why not?" She laughed as she recounted the story.

"What was the best part about being a bunny? Your parents' reaction?" Adam asked.

"Working at the Playboy Club. I financed my degree that way. That helped my parents understand what a good idea this was." She winked at Adam.

Adam thought of a million questions. What was Hefner really like? Would his third marriage ever go through? How does it feel to have all those eyes looking at you? Do you miss the excitement? Instead, he just sat and admired her. Wuss, he thought to himself. He didn't even mention that he'd once seen Christina's twelve year old Playmate of the Year centerfold at a friend's house.

Christina Montenegro knew her way around the Zona Rosa, visiting clothing boutiques and pointing out cafes she liked. Adam hated shopping, but this was like a magic show. Christina selected a blouse and skirt in one store and asked Adam what he thought of them when she modeled them.

Adam stammered, 'Nice!', and Christina bought them.

Afterward, Christina suggested lunch at El Sol, a trendy

Méxican restaurant with an immense wine selection, large aquariums, and a string quartet playing Spanish classical selections including *Granada* and *Andalucía* which capture the romance and passion of Spain. Later, they played contemporary Méxican pieces like Jennifer Pena's *Tuya*, and string interpretations of *Tengo Todo excepto a Ti* and *Bésame Mucho*. Adam loved the atmosphere. Rachel tapped out the Méxican songs with her freshman class ring on the table, lip synching the imaginary words, a product of having heard them in Spanish class many times.

After the two hour lunch that ended around 4 PM, they grabbed a taxi for Garibaldi Plaza in the center of México City. They were soon joined by Mrs. Fuller and Mrs. Snitterbank. After glasses of wine for the adults in an outdoor café fronting the plaza, Christina stood up and walked over to the nearest of at least fifty mariachi bands. Every eye watched her as she made that twenty step walk. When she returned, smiling, a group of eleven musicians followed her to the table, and sang and played *Guadalajara*, the signature piece for mariachi bands.

When the band finished and left, Rachel asked, "What do they charge, Christina, if I may ask?"

"The mariachis here are the best bargain in the world. I paid them five dollars but when I first came here the going price was only a dollar for a song. There've been price increases over the years. They play for less but I figure it's better to invest in the future of this music."

Adam then said, "And they divide that price eleven ways for the eleven man band. How late do they stay here and play?"

Christina responded, "As late as anyone wants to pay them. I arrived here once with Mr. Montenegro at 1 AM and spent three good hours with the bands going hard. You're looking at the renaissance

Garibaldi, though. This plaza went downhill for years but the government has done a complete restoration of the buildings and streets around the plaza. They've beefed up security, too." Adam glanced around and saw at least five blue suited policemen hanging around the shops and cafes.

Rachel said, "The drug culture has struck here, too, I'll bet." Christina nodded.

Mrs. Fuller, alarmed that the conversation was turning toward drugs, said, "The Tourism Board says the influence of drugs is greatly diminished in México City and will soon be throughout the country." Adam thought to himself that his Mom really doesn't believe that.

As if in answer to Adam's thought, Mrs. Fuller then changed the subject. "There's a restaurant near the hotel I'd like to suggest for dinner this evening around nine. Then to bed for an early start in the morning."

The five of them listened for awhile to the mariachis serenading couples. In one case, a group of eight American tourists really got into the music by standing up and dancing and had everyone in the Plaza cheering at the conclusion.

The following morning, Adam was up first, showered and dressed before he tapped Rachel on the arm. Rachel groaned and one eye popped open.

"Adam, what are you doing!" she shrieked.

"We've got fifteen minutes for you to shower and meet us in the lobby."

Rachel just made it.

The hour long trip to the pyramids thirty five miles to the northeast of México City was in fourteen seat tour buses each with a guide and a driver. There were eleven buses. The trip was made easier as this was Saturday morning with a minimal rush hour and took place before the large influx of tourists descended on one of the most fascinating monuments in México.

The tour guide talked most of the way, so by the time the party arrived at 10 AM, everyone on the bus understood the Teotihuacán culture. The guide intoned that the Teotihuacán civilization which lasted from 350 BCE through 950 CE succeeded the earlier Olmec dominance of México. The original city was culturally rich and strongly influenced by the contemporaneous Mayan culture further south. Human and animal sacrifice was practiced long before the Aztecs made these gruesome ceremonies standard fare starting in the 1250s CE. The Teotihuacánes developed extensive capability in the arts, economics and government. They integrated members of captured tribes into their society from throughout Mesoamerica, roughly today's México south to today's Costa Rica.

Teotihuacán art was influenced by the older Olmec civilization, especially as excavations at La Venta on the Méxican Caribbean coast demonstrated. Artwork included human figures, animal-human composites thought to be deities, axes and personal ornaments such as ear flares and beads. The art was small in scale and exhibited skilled command of the difficult-to-carve stone used.

The older Olmec jade art objects were translucent blue green in color and were never surpassed in the ancient Americas for compact, symmetrically balanced, three dimensional form and elegance of surface detail. The images were complex which added to their symbolic power and included birds and cats, especially jaguars.

The Moon Pyramid, one hundred sixteen feet high, is located to the north of the Avenue of the Dead, and the Sun Pyramid, the largest of three pyramids at two hundred sixty eight feet high, is near the southern end of the Avenue of the Dead. The third largest pyramid, the Pyramid of the Feathered Serpent or Quétzalcoatl, was completed later, about 200 CE, and is also in the south end of the city. There were two hundred human sacrifices buried under this pyramid and a tunnel sealed in 200 CE. The tunnel and burials under the pyramid were discovered recently by radar.

The city itself was huge for its day with many inhabitants living in the over two thousand apartments centered on the Avenue of the Dead.

The tour guide concluded her talk and the passengers sat quietly for the remainder of the trip.

The Avenue of the Dead, main street Teotihuacán, Mexico, with the 2000 year old Pyramid of the Sun in the center distance. The foreground structures along the Avenue are called platforms. Behind the camera is the smaller Pyramid of the Moon.

As the group left the buses and walked along the path toward the Pyramid of the Moon, Adam noticed the vendors. Two of the vendors offered tables and chairs carved from tan and white marble. Adam asked Mrs. Fuller if they could buy them and ship them back to decorate their backyard in San Diego. She declined. Soft drinks were offered at other stands. At one such stand, the owner demonstrated his donkey holding a soft drink bottle in its mouth and guzzling the drink down. Other stands sold CDs, straw hats, shirts with bits of wisdom printed on them front and back, like '*I Conquered the Teotihuacán Pyramids.*'

Rachel shouted to Adam, "Beat you to the top of the Moon!" and took off at run. Adam followed. They discovered that the steps were so high that climbing was a challenge more like rock climbing in the mountains of California, but without the pitons and safety equipment. They finally succeeded in getting to the top and waved back down at the three ladies they'd left behind.

The siblings, breathless, looked south down the Avenue of the Dead toward the dominant Sun Pyramid and the much smaller and newer Quétzalcoatl pyramid to the right and further south. Forgetting for a moment the missing wood and palm frond structures on the top where they stood - where human sacrifices had taken place - the siblings tried to comprehend the vista. Beyond were the immense mountains including the active volcano, Popocatépetl.

"This is one cool place, México. So much to see and absorb. Never guess this was here by walking the streets of Tijuana," Adam effused. Rachel nodded her agreement and started back down.

The group was back at the hotel in México City by 6 PM, well before the 9 PM dinner hour was to start. They took this time to swim in the hotel pool, an adventure Adam would not soon forget. Mrs. Montenegro had lost none of her earlier charm as a Playmate and every eye around the pool followed her, including Adam's. Rachel shot Adam a withering look.

The Sunday trip to Chapúltepec Park and the Museum of Anthropology took place during the midday hours. Adam, who didn't like museums, was blown away by this one nestled in the huge park with trees and vistas that include a large lake and a classy restaurant called Del Lago. Méxican history is displayed in the Museum of Anthropology that combines very high ceilings with open air architecture. Adam allowed he'd take a fresh look at museums from now on.

Mayan Exhibit, National Museum of Anthropology, Chapúltepec Park, México City, Courtesy of Wikipedia

Next morning they arrived early at the Benito Juárez International Airport for the trip home. Rachel, Adam and Mrs. Fuller rehashed their favorite parts of the adventure while Mrs. Montenegro and Mrs. Snitterbank visited the ladies room.

"Great trip, Mom. This is sure one time I'm glad you're a travel agent. México has such an immense and interesting history," Rachel enthused. "Too bad Adam couldn't keep his eyes off Mrs. Montenegro or he'd have gotten something out of the trip, too."

Adam glared at Rachel then smiled and said, "By keeping my eyes open, I learned more about México than you did, like Mrs. Montenegro looks OK modeling clothes, better in a bathing suit."

Then a voice in Spanish commanded everyone's attention before Mrs. Fuller could intervene.

"Attention!   Flight 212 to Tijuana now boarding at gate nineteen."

Mrs. Fuller arose from her seat pulling the small wheeled carry-on suitcase she called Quigley. She also carried a large plastic bag with handouts from the Méxican Tourist Bureau.

Georgia Snitterbank came out of the restroom and followed Mrs. Fuller to the gate. They'd planned to sit together on the way back to Tijuana International. Christina Montenegro arrived last and lined up with Rachel. They'd sit together on the way back.

Adam was odd man out.

Mrs. Fuller was a big fan of visiting new cities and would do so at the drop of a coin, often going on a moment's notice. México City had been fun for everyone in the group. "Georgia," she said, "I'm feeling a lot better about Adam taking this job with Méxican-American in Ensenada. They're so many good people in México." Their boarding passes were scanned and they proceeded down the ramp to the plane.

Once seated, Mrs. Fuller glanced around to see Rachel and Christina chatting away and Adam engrossed in the AeroMéxico magazine.

Georgia said, "Everything will be just fine for Adam."

"I agree. Now let's talk about the business for a few minutes. We just haven't had time."

Low commissions were forcing small travel companies out of business. Mrs. Fuller's *Great Escape* was still fairly strong, because she borrowed an idea from her family's travel business in New York

City, long since sold, which had emphasized packaged tours. As a result, her company was still a money maker.

"Georgia, on Tuesday we need to follow up with the Peterson's on their final plans for East Africa in July. They want something less fancy than the Norfolk Hotel in Nairobi."

"Already covered Jenny. I've booked them into the new Wakamba Lodge out toward the Rift Valley. I talked with Grace. She's just back from a visit there and says it captures the flavor of east Africa. The Petersons will have their own rondavel looking out over the valley." Grace was a much travelled friend of Georgia's.

"Rondavels. I would love to build one out near Palm Desert or maybe in Borrego Springs. A nice getaway for our best clients, low energy use with the thatched roof and straw bale walls. I'm sure I can convince Roger to go for it. A taste of Africa right here in San Diego County. What do you think?"

"I'd sure use it! Do it."

"All right then. Now give me the details on what the Petersons will have at Wakamba Lodge."

Georgia smiled and said, "Their rondavel has separate living room, kitchenette with breakfast nook, and bedroom with individual overhead fans, a bathroom with a garden view of the valley and massage jets in the tub. The room has a bar stocked with Kenya Cane rum, Rob Peterson's favorite. The dining room in the main building at the Lodge is huge and well-staffed for breakfast, lunch and dinner."

"Georgia, you're a genius."

"I wanted to tell you about it before I call the Petersons

tomorrow. Now what have you and Roger decided to do about Rachel and the U2 concert?"

"Rachel? You know she calls me the travel agent for guilt trips. I told her that I thought it was too big a risk to drive to Los Angeles less than a month into Mike Nelson's new driver's license. But Rachel is crazy about Mike. She figures if she turns him down, he'll disappear."

"She had some trouble getting over Dave Rydell, as I recall," said Georgia.

"Dave was her first boyfriend, the love of her life for six months. But Dave wanted more from Rachel than holding hands in the movies. I think Rachel was wise to put a stop to him when she did. Honestly, he wasn't good for her and it wasn't just the age difference."

"Dave was three years older than Rachel, as I recall. He could always get his hands on pot." Georgia remembered the details.

"When I found out about the pot, Rachel and I had our biggest fight ever. She told me, as angry as I've ever seen her, that Dave could also get Ecstasy faster than a wet house cat can run."

"Did Rachel do Ecstasy?"

"No, but she was sure evasive when I asked about pot."

"When my daughter went through that stage a few years ago, she said pot was medicinal, couldn't hurt anything."

"She might be right, except for jail time if you get caught breaking the Federal law that still pertains. Now Mike, in my motherly opinion, is a real catch. I've got to figure a way around this

U2 thing or Rachel may not speak to me again - ever."

The plane backed away from the gate and taxied out to the runway.

"Tell me more about Adam's job in México this summer," Georgia said, changing the subject.

"As you might guess, I wasn't thrilled about the job especially as Ensenada is so far into México. But I'm feeling good about it now. Adam will be driving a company pickup truck to shuttle people and parts back and forth between Ensenada and the truck depot south of town. He'll be an assistant to the fleet manager."

"That could be a fun job. Gets to meet new people, see a little of the countryside, try new restaurants."

"Roger thinks it's safe and the Montenegros are such careful and knowledgeable business people. Adam won't be on the produce delivery runs so he's at least that far removed from trouble."

Georgia said, "I've seen some of those Baja farms. They're big operations that grow tomatoes, peppers, grapes and melons. Adam could learn a lot about farming, too."

Jennifer agreed, "There are beautiful farms south of San Quintín, some four to ten thousand acres or more. Roger as you guess from hearing Christina talking about it knows both Miguel and Ricardo Montenegro really well. I've met them socially many times. They're great fun and both are very knowledgeable about many things, especially politics. Miguel, Ricardo's Dad, is classy and acts the role of senior statesman in the family. Ricardo has taken over running the company."

"Ricardo is probably good looking, too, judging from Christina," she said.

"No question about that," Jennifer said, winking at Georgia. "Ricardo took astronomy courses Roger taught at SDSU which is how we know Ricardo so well. Ricardo is apparently even better at running the business than his Dad was."

Georgia raising a new subject said, "I've not heard much about kidnapping in México lately."

Jennifer picked right up on that one. "Kidnapping is an issue. We have a Tijuana friend who heads the largest accounting firm in Baja California. The family has money and the business does well. Five members of his family have been kidnapped over the last ten years. In one case, our friend delivered a million dollars to the kidnappers to recover his cousin intact. The million dollars was gone. But it's been awhile since that happened. Seems quieter on the kidnapping front lately."

"Georgia said. "Where would anyone get a million dollars?"

"Came from credit lines in the business. Roger thinks the risks of kidnapping today are small. But I think I'd like a body guard for Adam this summer."

The plane accelerated swiftly down the runway and rose into the cloud-flecked sky, clear for once of the smog. México City's cleanup was working.

"Adam is so good looking. I'd volunteer to be his body guard in a heartbeat!" said Georgia, now laughing, herself a mother of a twenty four year old daughter.

Jennifer laughed, too, the tension and worry she felt gone. "I might just take you up on the offer!"

The Fullers arrived home in San Diego late Monday afternoon. Adam sensed that his mother was now OK with his summer job. Mission accomplished.

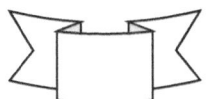

Chapter Seven
The Party
Sunday, June 1

Rachel said, "Can you believe Jason got caught stealing school computers last week?"

Adam and Rachel were sitting on the sofa in the living room at home talking about the latest development at Seaside. Adam had tried asking about Rachel's study breakfast with Mike Nelson that morning but had gotten nowhere.

Jason had big trouble with Mr. Volpini over classroom behavior. "Not surprised that he was behind a theft ring. I heard they sold four Seaside computers on eBay and Craigslist before they were nabbed," Adam responded.

Rachel said, "Jason got good grades but liked to cheat to see if he could get away with it. For him it was a game to play. Once he put a book up in front of his homework on his desk and was writing down the answers during the class discussion. Mr. V walked over and caught him at it. Jason showed no reaction at all to being caught. I think he's a sociopath."

"So when can we leave for the party?' Adam asked.

"Soon as I take my shower and get dressed," she said as she got up and ran down the hall to her room.

Later, Rachel glanced at her figure in the mirror as she stepped out of the shower. She turned sideways and tucked her tummy in. "Not bad," she said out loud. She'd already plucked her eyebrows which looked elegant, she noted. She worried that her nose was too small. Were her lips full enough? Maybe she should get collagen treatments. How would she get her Mom to go for that? Her mother wouldn't even let her buy the bathing suit she wanted last summer. A little heavier on the lipstick tonight, she concluded.

"I wonder if Mike's looking into his mirror right now," she said aloud, smiling. Rachel started to whistle *Norwegian Wood*, a song she liked from the Beatles CD birthday present she received in March.

The Sunday afternoon pool party would attract a lot of kids, Rachel knew. After all it was Memorial Day Weekend.

Kelsey Fortuna's twenty-five meter pool and Kelsey's parties were popular. Kids from other schools in town always showed up, too, invited or not. Kelsey had many friends through her outside theater activities. She'd been the star in Thornton Wilder's "Downtown" this spring which got good reviews in the *San Diego Union Tribune* newspaper. Kelsey's parents stayed to chaperone the parties, used the best catering services and hired a guard for the front door with a guest list. There'd be at least fifty kids there, Rachel thought. The pool, the view west across the north end of Mission Bay and the good food all promised an exciting party. The evening dance would add icing to the cake.

What *would* she wear, Rachel thought. Last summer's purple two piece bathing suit was shot and didn't fit that well anyway. She would be set for the dance with a ruffled white Méxican-style blouse with red stitching and tight black slacks she'd persuaded her mother to buy for her last week. That would be the bomb!

Maybe she should call Kira Alexander and borrow a bathing suit. Kira had more bathing suits than there were Cheerios in a cereal box. She and Kira were tall and wore the same sizes. They'd bailed each other out many times. Once they were shoe shopping together. Kira found a pair she liked. Rachel said to her that if that pair fits, get a pair in every color. They both laughed until tears ran. The salesman cracked up, too.

She called Kira from her cell phone and the deal was struck. Kira would bring the new bathing suit that Rachel liked best.

Rachel's real problem was Mike Nelson. The breakfast at Perry's Restaurant had gone pretty well, but by the time they all got to Mike's house, Rachel thought things were going downhill. Mike didn't seem as interested in her as he had. But then, she hadn't officially accepted his offer to the U2 concert either. Parents! They just DO NOT understand! At least, Rachel thought, Mike helped her get her arms around worldwide economic and political issues before World War II. She'd have preferred getting her arms around him.

Kira's loaner bathing suit would start drawing Mike back or she didn't know what would. Where was Adam? He should've been back from shopping with Mom long ago. Rachel blow dried her shoulder length brown hair then finished dressing.

Meanwhile, Adam turning into the Fuller driveway, said to his Mom, "Uh, oh! It's already three o'clock, the party is starting, I'm taking Rachel and I'm late. We have to stop on the way to pick up Julie."

"Here we are, Adam. Run in and get dressed. I'll get the groceries."

Rachel heard the car door slam then her Mom's unique laugh ringing out across the front yard. She ran outside to welcome her home.

"Tell me, Rachel, how did your breakfast with Mike go?" Mrs. Fuller bubbled as she grabbed an armful of groceries and carried them up the bricked front walk.

Rachel's good mood soured. "Awful! He paid no attention to me! You'd think since he asked me to the U2 concert next weekend, we could at least talk about something. No, he and Kira talked about the Lakers basketball game last weekend. I could barely eat my breakfast!"

Adam said, "I'll bet you studied some history with Mike, right?"

Rachel, now all worked up, ignored her brother's attempt at mollification, and Mrs. Fuller, well aware of Rachel's temper, was quiet, knowing what was coming.

As they closed the front door, Rachel said, "And I SUPPOSE you're going to let me go to that concert?" Rachel now suspected that Mr. V could bail her out, but she still hadn't heard back from him.

"Dear, let me unwind and put the groceries away first. We'll talk about it with Dad later tonight."

Rachel couldn't contain her emotions. "I knew it! You have no intention of letting me go!" said Rachel, as she steamed down the hall to her bedroom at the back of the house and once again slammed the door. When Rachel was little and confined to her bedroom for discipline, she liked to lie on her back on the bedroom floor and set up a steady patter by kicking the door with both feet. She didn't do that anymore but she still knew how to slam the door.

Adam spoke up. "Mom, that's not fair. Mike got one hundred percent on the written part of his driver's test and aced the in-car part, too. Besides, you know how Rach feels about U2. She'd walk to LA to see them if she had to!"

"We'll see, dear," Mrs. Fuller said, sounding too final. "We'll see."

"Mom, can I have one of those frozen Snickers bars?" Adam said, trying to fill the void created by Rachel's sudden departure and warm up the icy atmosphere.

"Only if you promise to eat your vegetables at dinner tonight. By the way, did I tell you that Georgia offered to guard you in México this summer? Wasn't that cute? I told her we'd talk about it and get back to her. Isn't she sweet?"

"Aw, Mom. You worry too much about me. Tell Georgia I'll be fine in México."

"I believe that, too, and of course I'm just kidding about hiring Georgia to follow you around. You'd better get dressed!   Be   home by eight. Dad and I have some news for you and Rachel."

Adam walked past Rachel's bedroom on the way to his own.

"Come on, Rach, or we'll be late to Kelsey's". He could hear a muffled sob from behind her door and knew she was in a twit about the concert.

"Leaving in ten minutes!" He quickly put on his blue Bermuda shorts and the white tank top that said 'Halsey' in big blue letters. Halsey was his favorite surfboard supplier. Adam liked surfing but hadn't found much time for it senior year.   Adam went out, started the Taurus and honked twice for Rachel.

On the way to get Julie, Adam said, "Rach, here's an idea. Why don't you let me drive you and Mike up to LA this weekend? You know, like your own personal chauffeur just for the two of you. I'll visit Brad up in Palos Verdes and pick you up after the concert. That would save you the hassle of dealing with the 'rents on Mike driving."

"Good grief, Adam! No way! How am I supposed to break that to Mike? 'Mike, the good news is I can go with you this Saturday, but the bad news is my Mom thinks you don't know how to drive, so my brother is going to drive us.' Thanks, Adam, but no thanks."

Julie Sandover was well-tanned this spring before anyone else.

She came out of her house on the run as Adam wheeled into the driveway, long hair up in a bun, wearing Carolina Herrera sunglasses, black Bermuda shorts, a black sleeveless blouse and black flip-flops

Adam jumped out, opened the front passenger side door, watching Rachel swing into the back seat behind him. He kissed Julie as she slid passed him and into the front seat. Adam said, "Hey, Kick, what's up! You look pretty classy." Adam called her Kick because of her ability to slam a soccer ball the entire length of the field. Julie and Rachel were both on the varsity team as juniors and sophomores, respectively.

"I was planning to wear my beach outfit, but there was a rip in it," she responded. "This is my fall back."

"You look perfect to me whatever you wear," Adam enthused.

"Julie, what movie did you two see last night?" Rachel probed, changing the conversation. Rachel liked Julie and wondered if Adam and Julie would stick together through college. Julie liked the idea of going to Washington, DC and Georgetown University the following year. But that would be a good eight hour bus ride from Dartmouth. And she had another year to go in San Diego where Dartmouth was a lot further than that. Adam hadn't had a girlfriend until his senior year and Rachel hoped Julie would work out.

Julie responded, "The one with Keanu Reeves and Drew Barrymore."

"I've heard about it. Was it any good?" Rachel asked as Adam pulled into traffic.

"Really sweet. The kissing scenes were terrific," Julie responded, glancing at Adam as she said it. "But the chase scenes are unbelievable and I think they turned the volume up too loud."

"I like the part where Reeves pulls Drew up the outside of the building to the roof to avoid the bacteria released inside by the terrorists," Adam interjected. Adam's fear of heights was operative here. But, perversely, Adam enjoyed watching others in a predicament he would have found impossible to endure himself.

By the time they arrived at Kelsey's, a fifteen minute drive, everyone in the car was feeling the excitement. Adam let the girls out at the door and headed off to find a parking place, difficult at best this close to Mission Bay.

Julie and Rachel went in past the guard, a well-tanned surfer dude taking a break from his passion to work this party. Kelsey came over and gave them each a hug.

"Hey, glad you're here. We've got a game of Slippery Fish going by the pool. Change in my bedroom." Rachel headed off to find Kira and get the promised bathing suit and Julie went straight into Kelsey's bedroom. Julie met Adam walking in the front door as she emerged.

"That was quick!" she said. "Thought you'd have to park in Clairemont and take a taxi back."

Adam said, "No sweat. Found a guy two blocks from here in a pickup just leaving his space and I grabbed it. Let's go see that game!"

Slippery Fish, sometimes known as Stinky Fish, or Red and Green Fish, had been this year's senior class favorite since eighth grade camp. The object of the game is to steal the fish from whoever is "it" for the game, by sneaking up behind "it", grabbing the fish and returning it to the starting line. The game always caused a lot of screaming and laughing and was a great way to start a party. Sarah Wolfe was "it" when Adam and Julie arrived. She defended the fish until time expired and won her game.

Adam then became "it." Adam had nowhere near Sarah's skills and was soon carted over to the pool and thrown in. He yelled, "This sucks!" as he hit the water upside down.

Slippery Fish ended when everyone jumped into the pool with Adam.

Rachel emerged in her "new" bathing suit minutes later. Adam noticed her arrival and whistled appreciatively and soon many of the other boys joined in the fun. Rachel, blushing, wanted to disappear, but instead walked over to the bar and grabbed a Pepsi.

Mike Nelson was soon by her side, and said, "Hi, glad you're here. Can you stay for the dance tonight?"

"Adam and I've got to leave early, but I'll be here for the start. Mike, sorry not to have gotten back to you about the concert next weekend, but I should have a definite answer tomorrow."

"Well, I've got the tickets and I've got the car."

Rachel, relieved that the dreaded subject was already out of the closet, was so excited to be with Mike that she thought her heart would explode.

"I'm really looking forward to going, Mike," she said. "And thanks again for sharing your history notes with me this morning. There is just SO much we need to know for the final." Rachel had a habit of emphasizing words in a certain way.

"Yeah, Wineheart covers the whole waterfront on his tests. It's never just 'analyze', it's always 'compare'. Tough. But I do like history, so if I can help more before Wednesday let me know." Mike put his arm around her and gave her a squeeze.

Rachel, heart pumping, just managed to say, "I appreciate it, Mike".

By now, a relay swimming race had started between three boys and three girls. Mike pulled Rachel over to watch. They ended up standing by Mr. Volpini.

Anthony Volpini's family emigrated from the Tuscan city of Bagnone, not far from Florence, in the 1960's. Volpini liked cooking Italian dishes, drinking Italian wine, and had a small Italian art collection, including one Caravaggio inherited from his grandfather. As a result of his popularity in the classroom, Volpini, known affectionately as "Mr. V", got invitations to student-organized events.

"Eh, Mike, what's up", Volpini said.

"Got my driver's license last week, Mr. Volpini," Mike glowed.

"How many trees have you killed so far, Mike?" Volpini loved poking fun at his students.

"Four, but none of them were my fault. Three stepped in front of me and the fourth was going to die anyway." Mike was well prepared for this teacher. He thought about the time Mr. Volpini grabbed him in eighth grade class, turned him upside down, and shook him until coins dropped out of his pockets. Then Volpini had said, "Thanks for the tip," and turned him over again. Volpini had played football, weighed close to two hundred and eighty pounds and was still easily able to hoist a then much smaller Mike Nelson.

"What's new in science, Mr. V?"

"We started the robot program this spring in ninth grade. The robots roamed around the science quad, gathered temperature data and brought it back."

"Cool. I heard about it. One of the 'bots took a wrong turn, so I was told, and fell over the cliff. Did you ever get that one back?" Mike asked, a grin at the corner of his mouth. The Seaside High School campus covered twenty two acres on top of a mesa overlooking Mission Valley so there were cliffs to take into consideration.

"No, the robot never came back." Volpini leaned in toward Mike, assuming a conspiratorial air. "As far as I know, it was last seen retrieving golf balls from the lake on the golf course. Pay was better than taking temperature measurements for Seaside High School science students." Mike laughed, decided to give it a rest and moved away to get a better view of the race in progress, now in its second lap.

The boys had spotted the girls one length of the pool in a six length race and were now trying to catch them, each competitor would swim two lengths except the first girl to swim.

Mr. Volpini watched too, knowing the finish would likely be close. Adam was the last boy to swim. He was lining up on the pool edge to go. Julie stood beside him, a good swimmer, competitive at everything she did, who was also swimming anchor.

"Adam, you haven't got a chance!" Volpini yelled across the water.

"Watch that kind of talk. I'll see you after the race." Adam actually would be pleased if Julie won, but would try his best to see that didn't happen. Julie made a perfect flat dive as her teammate finished her leg and touched the wall. Now Adam knew it would be close. The girls had an eight second lead as Adam dove into the pool. He was a strong swimmer and was coming into the wall as Julie did her flip and headed down the stretch. Adam's turn wasn't his best. Now the crowd got into the race, shouting in unison, "Warm up the bus!" This chant was used at Seaside High School athletic events to let the visiting team know what Seaside students thought of the visiting team's chances of a victory. In this swimming race, of course, it didn't matter who was favored, the chant still applied.

After the race, which the girls won by the length of a hand, Adam came over to Mr. Volpini, and said, "You put something in the water, Mr. V!"

"You didn't feel that rope around your ankles? Seriously, you fellows are in real trouble if these ladies can whip you that easy!"

The smell of grilling burgers wafted across the yard. Adam left to collect Julie and get something to eat. While Julie favored veggie burgers, Adam was the world's biggest hamburger fan. He could down a six-by-six. Adam remembered for an instant the time that Mr. Fuller tricked Rachel and Adam with ostrich burgers. Mr. Fuller ordered ostrich meat from Jonathan's Market, had some of it ground up for burgers, served the kids "hamburgers" and asked how they were. "Great," they each responded. Then Mr. Fuller said, "Really? Those were actually ostrich burgers!"

Rachel then grabbed her throat, gagged and shouted, "I'll never eat anything you serve again!" and ran out of the dining room. Rachel didn't like eating birds.

Mr. Fuller, not the least upset, had laughed and said since they apparently couldn't tell the difference, he would always serve ostrich burgers from now on. Ostrich meat was low in fat, high in protein, and tasted like beef.

Adam wondered what had happened to ostrich meat after all of the hype about it a few years back.

Later, when the music began to roll, Rachel danced non-stop with Mike for half an hour. But she and Adam had to leave the party early, dropping Julie at her home on the way. Rachel was more than a little upset over leaving the dance.

As they pulled into the Fuller driveway, Adam said, "At least you got to dance with Mike, Rach. He liked your bathing suit, didn't he?"

"He would've if I'd been there long enough!" Rachel snapped back.

"What do you think Mom and Dad want to talk about?" Adam asked.

As the pair entered the house, Mrs. Fuller said, "Right on time. Extra credit. Come on into the living room and we'll tell you what this is all about."

Mr. Fuller broke the news. "I'm able to get time off from work in August so we'll take the boat to Catalina. We'll be there the week before Adam leaves for college. You both get to bring a guest." The Fuller's owned a 1965 Kettenburg 43, a forty three foot long classic wooden sailboat.

Rachel envisioned showing Mike Two Harbors, the rustic town on the northwest end of the island, Cherry Cove just to the north and

Emerald Bay with a small rocky crag just offshore that still technically belongs to Spain. It'd been left off the map transferring ownership from Spain to the U.S.

Santa Catalina Island is immortalized by The Four Preps in the song "*Twenty six Miles Across the Sea*", the approximate distance of the island from the nearest point on the southern California mainland. From San Diego, the trip was seventy miles and usually involved a stop-over in Dana Point on the way. Rachel was suddenly feeling much better about life.

"OK if I bring Julie?" Adam asked with a wink.

"In order to put this together, Adam has to get off from his job at Méxican-American a week early. I've asked Ricardo Montenegro and that will be OK with him," Mr. Fuller added.

Rachel said, "Great Mom, thanks Dad, I'm really looking forward to Catalina. But I thought this meeting was to be about THE CONCERT."

Mr. Fuller quickly responded, "It is. We want you to go to the concert. But not with Mike driving. We could offer to take you, but I've got to speak at the SDSU fund raiser Saturday night and your Mom needs to be with me."

Mrs. Fuller said, "So, Georgia Snitterbank has offered to be your personal chauffeur."

Rachel screamed, "NO WAY! You know how I feel about HER." Georgia had been her baby sitter once. Rachel and Georgia had a pitched battle over inviting her best friend over for the night. Rachel still felt her face flush when she thought about it. "Now, if you'll excuse me, I'm meeting Mr. V early tomorrow in the science lab."

"Dear, we'll talk about this again."

"Again will be too late, Mother," Rachel shouted as she disappeared toward her room.

"What's Rachel doing now in science lab?" Mr. Fuller asked, turning to Adam.

Adam responded, "Rachel's part of the group doing a tune-up for the lab final." Adam glanced at Mrs. Fuller. He'd not yet told his parents they'd discovered cocaine in the Cuyamaca white powder earlier in the week. But they seemed OK with his explanation about what Rachel was doing. Sooner or later he'd tell them. Maybe when he knew what the powder meant.

Mrs. Fuller walked back to Rachel's bedroom door. "Rachel," she said. "We'll find a way to get you to the concert that works for everyone. Good night, dear." Nothing came back.

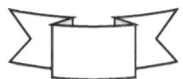

Chapter Eight
Ensenada
Tuesday, June 3

The movie *Conejo de la Luna* was presented during the AP Spanish Cultural History review class Monday because the teacher was out. Substitute teachers often receive lesson plans to show a movie, nothing more. Just take attendance, turn out the lights and enjoy.

Adam sat with Julie in the class even though he'd already taken the AP exam for Spanish, so was finished with high school Spanish. He and Julie talked about the movie after class. Both thought the story was rough, the gratuitous violence and sex out of control. Julie admired the acting. They both agreed the scene with the heroine peeing her pants was crude.

Adam argued that playing the movie to high school students challenged constitutional First Amendment limits on freedom of speech. He said at least some form of parental approval should be required before teachers showed this kind of four-letter-word studded creation to high schoolers. Adam in his mind was protecting his little sister Rachel with this argument. He would never have asked for parental approval for himself unless forced into it.

But Adam found an important personal message in the movie: *be careful whom you trust.* In the film, the politicians, businessmen and police of modern day México are influenced by issues other than running the country, building industry, or keeping order on the streets. Greed, wealth and power became motivating forces for some who start out their careers with purer purposes in mind.

The movie was still in the back of Adam's head the next morning, a sunny Tuesday, as he dropped Mr. Volpini and Rachel at Seaside High School. Volpini's gray Thunderbird coupe was in the shop for a clutch, so Adam gave him a ride to school, too. Mr. V shared donuts.

"Thanks for the donut, Mr. V," Adam shouted pulling away from the Seaside drop off zone in the family Taurus. "I'm off to México!"

Adam drove south through San Diego on Interstate 5, his México-American Freightways folder tucked into his briefcase in the trunk. Adam felt excited and adventurous.

Rush hour traffic going south to the border was light, unlike the three hour border jam coming north. Adam was red lighted at the border and had to go through inspection. The Méxican inspectors were quick and efficient and he was on his way in minutes. Inspections going into México usually looked for cash - drugs north, cash south.

Rounding the looping turn toward Highway 1, Adam merged quickly with traffic and sped through Tijuana easily. As he drove, he thought about the contrasts in fast-growing Tijuana: the Plaza de Toros Monumental de Tijuana bull fighting ring by the romantic beaches known as Playas de Tijuana; the Tijuana Cultural Center, a large round ball of a building, with museums, music, art, dance and an IMAX; world class restaurants like Cien Años where the menu includes recipes from one hundred years ago; many colleges and universities; the new Business Innovation and Technology Center; the increasingly high tech *maquiladora* manufacturing base. And the largest, most appalling slum found in North America, a city with drug and kidnapping gangs running wild, with shootouts between gangs on the streets which contained pockets of extreme poverty.

Adam veered around a truck that was pulled off the access road to change a tire.

Highway 1 is a well-marked four lane, black topped road with whitewashed culverts along both sides and a panoramic view of the Pacific Ocean. The tolls are payable in U.S. or Méxican currency, the lines short and traffic usually moves right along. At Rosarita, Adam passed the exit that leads to El Nido –The Bird's Nest – a rustic local bar with bamboo wood ceiling and a patio out back with active birds' nests everywhere. Adam made a mental note to stop there on the way north in the afternoon and say hello to the bar tender, Max. Max made the best margaritas south of the border. After all, Adam was now employed, had achieved the drinking age of eighteen in México, and was about to enjoy some of the perks.

Ensenada is a quieter, smaller town of just over a quarter of a million souls, one seventh the size of Tijuana. Salsipuedes Bay and Todos Santos Island just off Ensenada offer eye-popping views west from downtown Ensenada. Surfers love the thirty foot waves that break onto Todos Santos. Visitors wouldn't miss Hussong's Cantina or Papas and Beer for a tequila shooter or two and a mariachi band to play favorite songs for a few dollars each. The main street, Adolfo Lopez Mateos, features colorful shops and fish taco stands.

Looking south toward Ensenada's Salsipuedes Bay from Highway 1. Author photo

The El Rey Sol Restaurant in Ensenada is popular with locals. This oldest pastry shop in town was started many years ago by a tiny, vivacious lady named Doña Pepita, beloved by all who knew her. The bakery has expanded more recently into an award winning French restaurant.

Adam arrived in Ensenada an hour after starting his journey and turned left onto a side street. Méxican-American's offices were spiffy and new and just around the corner from the Santo Tomas Winery and restaurant. Adam parked on the street and walked up to the second floor offices.

"Good morning, Adam, welcome to Méxican-American," a dark haired, fair skinned beauty greeted him effusively from behind the polished wood receptionist's desk. "My name is Sonia Vidaña."

"Sonia, good to meet you. I guess Mr. Montenegro warned you that I'd be here today." This is someone I could really get to like, Adam thought to himself. If only I didn't already have a girlfriend.

"Have you been to Ensenada before?" she asked.

"I came once with the family of my best friend and we stayed at a hotel on Estero Beach. Rode horses along the beach."

"That's a lot of fun, isn't it? I'll be your concierge this summer if you have questions about Ensenada. This is my home town." She paused and said, "Mr. Montenegro just called. He'll be here in a few minutes. There was a meeting at our truck depot first thing and it ran longer than planned. Drug inspections to protect our trucks aren't easy to implement." Adam reflected that trucks going north to the States with produce were easy targets for drug traffickers to use as carriers. Preventing unwanted piggyback cargo was a headache.

"Would you like a coffee while you wait?" Sonia asked. Adam had grabbed a Power Bar on the way out the door at home, Mr. V's donut was long gone and he was feeling a growling in the belly.

"Sonia, you can read my mind. Sure!"

"Bet you want cookies with the coffee, Adam. Right?" she asked, her black eyes flashing. Cookies were a Méxican tradition. Sonia had the drop on him.

"Perfect, Sonia."

Sonia returned with a tray of coffee and cookies.

Adam grabbed two cookies and held one in each hand. "Sonia,

this is what I call a balanced diet."

Sonia laughed.

Adam continued, "I just read an article about that family gunned down north of town near the El Sauzal community."

"Adam, it was awful. Nineteen people were killed four years ago, all members of the same family. I knew the daughter of the owner of the ranch, Mariela Colón. We went to high school here together, same class," Sonia said, as she poured the coffee and set the rest of the cookies on the short table in front of Adam. "Mariela was very smart and beautiful, too. She finished third in the Miss Ensenada pageant at the San Nícolas Hotel her senior year in high school. I thought she'd win, but she never smiled for the entire contest – she didn't really want to win. Her father had insisted she enter. What a tragedy. I miss her."

"Payback," Adam said. "I'll bet it was a turf war. They waited until the family reunion at the ranch then struck."

"It was over late payments. Something like three million dollars. Still no arrests have been made. Fingers are pointing to the Arturo Acevedo Tijuana drug gang. Adam these Tijuana guys are scary!"

Adam, trying to lighten the mood, responded, "My Dad always says if everything seems to be going well, you've obviously overlooked something, like late payments." Sonia didn't react, trying to make sense out of what Adam said. Language barrier.

The door opened suddenly and Adam almost jumped out of his seat as Mr. Montenegro entered. Why was he on edge over a little drug war, Adam asked himself.

"Good morning, Adam. Nice of you to come a week early. I like your enthusiasm."

"Just want to get the paperwork out of the way and see what else I can do, Mr. Montenegro. I've got time this week between clearing out my locker at school and the senior parties."

"I forgot about the parties." Montenegro winked at Sonia. "I know you're already accepted at Dartmouth. Takes a load off. So congratulations again, Adam, you'll have a good time there. Good morning, Sonia," Montenegro said, turning to her. "Black coffee please, hold the cookies. Adam, come into my office and we'll discuss your job. Then stop by Personnel. Félix Delgado will give you a tour of the truck depot afterwards."

"Cool," Adam responded as they entered Montenegro's spacious office with a view of the waterfront.

"Now Adam, tell me how your father is doing. I haven't seen him since late last year, although we've spoken on the telephone several times."

"You've heard about the new telescope being planned for Mt. Laguna. This'll put San Diego State astronomy on the map. Dad has been making presentations to potential donors. It's going well and he said yesterday the campaign will go over the top this summer. Then construction can start in the fall. How is your father?"

"He's slowing up a bit at seventy five. He visits the property our family owns in Michoacán. That's where we're from. He's now trustee emeritus for San Diego State. When he was more active as trustee, he helped find and hire your Dad into the astronomy department."

"Yep. And you took Dad's course there."

"Ended up taking two courses with him. He's a crazy man with a white board and a Magic Marker. That's why I often go back to campus. The connections, the memories, the football and basketball games. Aztec blood runs deep in our family."

This dude looks like a movie star, Adam thought, watching him sip his coffee. A photo of his wife, Christina Montenegro, sat prominently on his desk.

"Did Mrs. Montenegro tell you about our adventures in México City?" Adam asked.

"Yes. I'm glad she could go. She loves México." His response showed how proud he was of her. "Adam, please ask your father to call me about his fundraiser. Business has been good. I'd like to help him out. We've just landed a contract from Empresas Piña to ship all their products from San Quintín to Los Angeles. Big contract, lots of competition, lots of pineapples. I think the deciding factor was that we committed to use new trucks for them. We'll have to buy six new trucks." But Montenegro smiled as he said it.

"I'll tell Dad tonight. Thanks for the offer to help."

"You're welcome, Adam. Now let's get down to business. Your position is a new one reporting to Mr. Delgado. He started as a driver sixteen years ago and is now in charge of our entire fleet of trucks and drivers. Last week, after discussions with the U.S. Drug Enforcement Administration and the México Federal Police we've agreed to increase surveillance of our own truck fleet. You may not have heard, but one of our drivers was suspended two weeks ago pending an investigation. A routine stop by México drug authorities found a magnetic box attached to the chassis of his truck at the

Mexicali check point. He may be innocent but the company is liable, so we're as interested in the matter as the Méxican local and federal police."

"Mr. Montenegro, I don't see how I can help you. I have no experience with drugs. You need a private investigator skilled in drug shipments," Adam said. "Besides, I thought my job would be assisting Mr. Delgado with shipments and driving truck parts around."

"Things have changed since earlier this spring, Adam. We need to focus our resources on the drug issue. Adam, you bring a dimension to our company that's missing. You're an excellent science student and you have an interest in computers and the internet. You can research the problem we face and look for commercially available solutions to help us protect ourselves. Or perhaps suggest that we design our own unique solutions like audio and visual detectors, drug sniffers, who knows what, to help solve this problem."

"OK, I'm with you. I make a presentation of my research to you and Mr. Delgado, with recommendations to protect your entire fleet of trucks from trouble, especially drug traffickers. I know I can help you do that, Mr. Montenegro. Let's move my start date up to today!" Adam was almost bouncing in his seat thinking about the new challenges. And his parents would be happy to learn that Adam would be doing more think tank work and less operations work.

"Done, Adam. Let's get you down to Personnel. I'll ask Sonia to call Mr. Delgado to meet you here and take you on a tour of the truck depot. I believe you'll be impressed."

Adam completed the visit to Personnel, a one man office just down the hall from Montenegro's office, then met Delgado out front.

"Let's go, Adam," Félix exclaimed when they met. "We'll take my pickup."

They talked baseball as they drove out of downtown Ensenada and passed the entrance to *La Bufadora*, one of three marine geysers in the world. Adam made a mental note to stop in to see this eighty foot high geyser on one of his visits to Ensenada this summer.

Félix quoted statistics on how National and American league teams were doing. He seemed to favor the San Diego Padres, though, and Adam knew a fair amount about the home team, so could keep up his end of the conversation. The drive to the truck depot south of town took only twenty minutes, not long enough to get much beyond the current baseball season.

The truck sheds were open air. The metal roof structure was covered by lightweight corrugated, translucent fiberglass roofing panels, protecting the vehicles parked within from the scorching sun. Adam wondered aloud how the trucks were maintained in such fine shape.

"We wash and polish the trucks and trailers in the last station to your right once a week, unless a customer job prevents it. A three man crew takes two hours to clean a big rig. We have a hundred thousand dollar automatic cleaning system but we hand wipe the vehicles down after washing, vacuum them out, Armor All the interiors, and dress the tires. The system recycles water which keeps the cost down. As a result, our fleet always looks good on the road. Appearance is important to our customers and prospective customers. After all, their company names are on the trailers. We also do mechanical, tire, cosmetic and fluid replenishment checks after every job, on a schedule we developed from recommendations by the truck vendors. We do mechanical repairs ourselves using the working pits to your right."

"Why?" Adam asked.

"Good question. First, we get better work from our staff than we would from an outside supplier. Second, we can do emergency turnaround much faster. We set our own priorities. Since engine overhauls need to be in a clean environment, that work is done in the white shed on the other side of the pits. The shed is air conditioned in the summer and heated in the winter and has excellent lighting. We also have a paint shop just around the corner. We paint on the company or customer logos there and touch up dings in the body work."

Adam was impressed. "I understand from Mr. Montenegro that you're buying new trucks for the Piña contract. Lots of new logos to paint. How many mechanics do you have?" he asked.

"We're buying six new tractors and ten trailers for that contract. That's thirty two logos, as a matter of fact. And to answer your question, we have two factory trained full time mechanics, one for Ford and one for GM, the two brands of trucks we own. However, both men can work on either brand. We also subcontract some work out to local shops we trust if we're very busy."

"Impressive" said Adam.

"Now," said Félix, turning toward Adam, "let's drive down to San Quintín for lunch. I'll introduce you to one of our biggest customers. Then you'll want to head home. The post 9/11 San Ysidro border wait going north is tough."

The pair got back in Delgado's pickup and again headed south. The road was like driving through Big Sur in central California, south of Monterrey. In both cases, narrow, twisty roads offer spectacular vistas and huge drops to the ocean at Big Sur and to verdant valleys and farms on the way to San Quintín.

Suddenly, Adam exclaimed, "Look! A car at the bottom of the cliff!"

A burned out car stood at the bottom of a five hundred foot drop from the road to the floor of the valley, still on its wheels. All the glass was gone, the roof and fenders crunched.

"Sad ending for a fine car," Delgado said. "Either going too fast, had too much to drink, or both. Or maybe this was retribution."

"What do you mean by retribution?"

"Let's say somebody wants to settle a score or make a statement. He might borrow a car, take it for a little ride and push it off a cliff down here," Delgado smiled, looking at Adam.

"Wow that sucks!   Pays to keep your nose clean, doesn't it?"

"Adam, sometimes even minding your own business doesn't help." Adam felt a chill run down his spine.

Just then they rounded a corner. The land flattened out in front of them clear to the horizon. The most beautiful vineyard Adam had ever seen stretched out to the east, toward the rising sun. The fence posts supporting the vines were in lines as straight as arrows. The grape vines grew exceptionally large and healthy leaves. There were no weeds between rows of plants in the freshly turned, rich, reddish brown soil.

"These farms are incredible," Adam said.

"The farms are large and productive," Delgado said, showing pride in his country's agricultural achievements. "You'll find farms here between five hundred and four thousand acres. Further south they get even bigger. There's good water and the soil is well suited to a variety of crops. Having the Pacific Ocean nearby keeps the temperature mild – in the seventies and eighties, unlike the east coast of Baja California, which swelters at a hundred and ten degrees in the summer. That side of Baja is a desert. No water except by irrigation."

"I've been there. Lots of sand and cactus. In fact, we actually drove on part of the Baja 1000 off road race course near San Felipe once. That's rough!" Adam exclaimed.

"You're right. But that's the idea."

"I cannot imagine doing that race on a motorcycle." But you could tell Adam thought he might like to try it, just once, by the way he moved around in his seat and looked directly at Delgado.

"Four wheels just make more sense sometimes, right?" Delgado said.

"Right. Like on these narrow roads," Adam said, feeling uneasy with the lack of guard rails on the highway to San Quintín.

Then Delgado continued his pep talk on Baja farms. "Now, the big money crops from San Quintín farms are tomatoes, peppers, and more recently, grapes. You'll see some melon farming, too. These farms keep our trucks very busy."

A half an hour later, they slowed and turned right into an unpaved parking lot. "Adam, we'll stop here at *Compañias Ferrér* on the way to lunch at my favorite restaurant. The founder's son, José, is a good friend of mine. José has just become president of the family business so we hope to continue our good relationship with them. I'll bring him out to the car. Wait here."

Delgado disappeared into a dusty looking two story building. A faded logo of a bald eagle was displayed over the red lettering of *Compañias Ferrér* on the side of the building. The cars and pickup trucks in the lot looked dusty too. Adam reflected that one of the major products from these farms is dust. Here was the proof.

When Delgado emerged from the building, Adam was surprised to see that Delgado's friend José Ferrér was fair skinned, blonde and blue eyed.

"Adam, please meet Mr. Ferrér."

"My pleasure, sir," Adam responded, shaking Ferrér's hand.

Ferrér, noticing Adam's eye on Ferrér's impressive head of hair, said, "In case you're wondering, my mother is German. I got her hair genes, not my father's. He's Méxican. Our business is fifth generation family owned and run. I'm the first to bring German efficiency into play." Ferrér said this with a twinkle in his eye. Delgado laughed.

"Don't be misled, Adam. Compañias Ferrér has long had a history of excellent management and superior performance," Delgado informed Adam.

"Thank you, Félix, for the kind words. Are we going to Doña Inéz' restaurant for lunch?" Ferrér asked.

"Does the sun come up in the east? Yes, sir, Don José, for sure," said Félix Delgado, using the local term of respect for addressing important persons.

They drove rapidly south discussing farming issues and telling stories. An hour passed pleasantly.

Ferrér spoke up as the car slowed on the main road at the only stop light in sight. "Adam, I'll tell you a story as we wait for the light to change. Two years ago this month, I was approaching this same light in my pickup as the light turned red. Suddenly, a car swerved in front of me and stopped. Thinking this looked like trouble, I immediately tried to back up. But a truck had pulled in right behind me. Four men jumped out of the car in front, carrying AK-47 assault rifles. I was given no choice but to join them in their car. The car had no license plate so there was no way I could later track them. I was kidnapped! A one million dollar ransom note was delivered to my family. The happy ending is that my family raised the money and I was released in one piece." Ferrér's forehead glistened with sweat as he relayed this experience and recalled the terror.

"Mr. Ferrér, that's awful. Did the police catch them?" Adam asked.

"No, Adam, they're still out there somewhere. Sad to say, this kidnapping business is a way of life in México. The federal police now have a special task force. We think kidnapping will be under control in a few years. Ah, and now you'll meet Doña Inéz herself, one of God's gifts to the restaurant business."

Delgado drove into the restaurant parking lot. Adam noticed his normally strong appetite had disappeared with José Ferrér's kidnapping story and didn't improve much over lunch as Ferrér spun his fascinating farming tales.

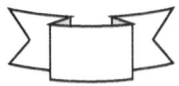

Chapter Nine
Family Dinner
Tuesday, June 3

Dinner at the Fuller home that night was pork chops, rice seasoned with garlic and herbs, and a tossed green salad with blue cheese dressing. Definitely a favorite of Adam's.   He used more barbecue sauce on his pork chops than everyone else combined.

Mr. Fuller said, "Tell us about México today, Adam."

"Mr. Montenegro says hello. He's moved my start date up to today. And get this: he says he'll contribute to your fund for the new telescope. He says business is exceptionally good right now and he wants to help."

"I thought he might want to contribute, but I couldn't ask him because he'd already given you a job this summer. You hate to ask a friend for too much. How were the people you met?"

"His office assistant, Sonia Vidaña, is cool. She gives me cookies."

"Adam," Rachel interjected. "I'm telling Julie."

"Cool it, Rach, Sonia is twenty." She was actually not yet twenty.

"I'm not sure that would stop you," she continued, scowling with fake indignation.

"Rach, should I mention Paul or Eduardo?" Adam shot back, a reference to older men Rachel had admired in their earlier adventures in France and Ecuador. Mrs. Fuller raised her eyebrows; Mr. Fuller was as usual, oblivious. "And I really like Félix Delgado," Adam continued, recovered from Rachel's attack. "He knows a lot about baseball, so we talked baseball. He memorizes batting averages. Then he showed me through their truck depot. They do most of their work on the trucks in-house. Finally, he introduced me to one of their biggest customers, Compañias Ferrér. I work directly for Mr. Delgado."

"Good," Mr. Fuller said. "What's your job going to be? Expediting?"

"The job's changed. Mr. Montenegro has asked me to do a science and technology survey. Recommend equipment and precautions to stop the piggy back drug shipments on the trucks coming north." Adam noticed a pleased expression appear on his mother's face with this news. Then he continued, "They've had one drug incident in the last two months and are worried about more." Mrs. Fuller again looked worried. Adam skipped telling about the burned out car and Ferrér's kidnapping. Bad timing. More secrets he couldn't tell his parents, he thought. He glanced at Rachel to see if somehow she guessed there was more to the story and that Adam was covering up. She was looking right at him.

Adam wiped the barbecue sauce from his chin.

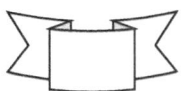

Chapter Ten
The Concert
Friday and Saturday, June 6 and 7

Rachel couldn't concentrate. She sat in class thinking about riding with Mike in the back seat of Mr. Volpini's gray Thunderbird all the way to the U2 concert.

Mme. Peterson said "Rachel" a second time.

"Yes, Madame P," Rachel said, snapping back to reality.

"Rachel, welcome back. Now what did William the Bastard do to Harold of England to seal Harold's fate?" The class had spent the spring reading about the Norman invasion of England in 1066 C.E. in French. This was sure to be at least one of the questions on the final next week. Rachel had a leg up for the final since she'd visited Bayeux in Normandy, France in December with her travel agent mother, who'd explained everything.

Rachel responded, "William tricked Harold by hiding a saint's relics under a cloth on the table when Harold swore fealty to William. William had saved Harold from a band of bounty hunters and paid a princely sum for Harold's release. Now the oath – taken on the saint's bones – could never be broken, or dire consequences for Harold would result. Harold could never go against William." Phew, thought Rachel, dodged that bullet! But William was not so constrained by the relics to go against Harold, and he did so in the Battle of Hastings in 1066, Rachel said to herself finishing the answer.

Mme. Peterson said, "OK, class, let's end today on that note. Tomorrow we'll cover the issues surrounding the Bayeux tapestry which explains the Norman invasion of England from the French point of view. Dismissed."

On the way out the door, Kira said, "You escaped that one by the skin on your teeth."

"You could tell I wasn't there today?"

"Mme. Peterson sure did. Date with Mike, right? By the way, my bathing suit looked great on you at Kelsey's party last weekend. Or was it that you looked great in my bathing suit? Mike couldn't keep his eyes off you."

"The suit was perfect. All I could think about in class today is whether Mr. V gets the tickets so Mike and I can drive with him."

"Sounds like fun, Rach. Call me tonight and let me know whether it's a go."

Mr. Volpini's classroom was the usual after school bustle as Rachel came in the door. Equations all over the board. Chemistry at its best. Questions flying from the students there for the review. Mr. Volpini spotted Rachel and winked at her. Rachel knew instantly he had the tickets.

"Mr. Volpini, you got them!"

"Yep. Let's plan on meeting at your house at 2 PM Saturday. I know a nice Italian place where we can stop for dinner along the way. Can you get Mike to your house Saturday? It'll simplify logistics."

"Oh, thanks, Mr. V. You bet we'll be ready."

Rachel found Mike in Mr. Wineheart's classroom. "Any chance you could give me a lift home today, Mike? Adam is in Ensenada."

"Love to. Meet me at the car in twenty minutes."

On the way home with Mike, Rachel said, "Mike, I'd love to accept your invitation to the concert."

"Too late, Rachel, I've already asked Sarah." Rachel's eyes grew large. Sarah would be really bad news. "Just kidding, Rach. Great you can go! When can I pick you up?"

"Mike, my parents are totally nuts about me and the freeway. Mr. V has volunteered to drive us and pick up the gas and the parking. My parents think that would be great."

"You mean we'd be stuck in the back seat of that car all the way up there?"

"Kinda."

"Rad. My parents don't like me driving the freeway, either. This will take some heat off me at home."

Rachel was recovering from a near heart attack. Sarah Wentworth was definite competition. But she said excitedly, "Mr. V has offered to show us how to eat Italian food on the way. If we leave by 2 PM Saturday, we can eat and be early to the concert."

"Mr. V really goes out of his way for you."

"I covered for him once or twice so his girlfriend Katie Rogers wouldn't know he was breaking his diet. Caught him eating desert at an Italian restaurant. Plus, he can't fool me with his trick science questions in class." The car arrived at the Fuller driveway.

"Thanks for the ride, Mike. See you tomorrow." Rachel kissed Mike on the cheek, jumped out of the car and ran into the house.

Her Mom was home early.

"Good heavens, Rachel, I haven't seen you this excited since we got you a tricycle when you were three."

Rachel explained the developments.

"But sweetheart, your father and I wanted to invite you and Mike to the SDSU astronomy department banquet Saturday night. You can go to that concert any old time." Rachel was used to her mother's sense of humor and simply smiled at the attempted joke.

"Wonderful news, Rachel," Jennifer continued, relieved that the major family crisis of the year had been averted.

Rachel immediately raised a serious issue. "Oh, wow, Mom, now I have to figure out what to wear." That issue took some time to resolve.

On Saturday, Mr. V pulled into the Fuller driveway at 2 PM on the dot. Mr. Fuller came out first and greeted Tony with a grin.

"Are you and Katie going to be able to keep an eye on this pair tonight?"

"You bet! The twelve inch rule does it every time." Tony was referring to his fondness for using a foot long ruler to separate slow dancers at teacher chaperoned Seaside parties.

"I'd invite you in, but I know you're anxious to get going. Rachel is still putting the final touches on her outfit. Mike is here. Hope you all have a great time tonight."

As Mr. Fuller headed back into the house, Mike and Rachel came out. Mike was in sports shirt and slacks, but Rachel was wearing a short black dress that definitely emphasized the positives. The head of the Seaside Middle School, seeing a dress like this one on Rachel for eighth grade promotion, commented that Rachel needed suspenders. Not to hold the dress up, but to hold it down. Who knows how Rachel got a dress this short past her fashion policewoman mother.

"Our reservations at Santa Lucía are for 5 PM so we should move right along," Mr. Volpini said as they turned onto the freeway.

Glancing in the rear view mirror, he noticed that the twelve inch rule was already being broken.

"If you two can stay a reasonable distance apart back there, I'll spring for double on the desserts," he said mashing the throttle to get up to the 85 MPH it took just to stay even with traffic. "Katie, you're in charge of music."

Inserting a CD, Katie said, "No desserts for you, big boy. Will you two in the back go along with the Beatles Number One hits? It'll get us into the right frame of mind for fast lane changes."

"Sounds good to me," Rachel and Mike said in unison and both laughed.

The Saturday evening crowd at Santa Lucía's had not yet arrived. The wine was first on the agenda. Mr. V ordered two different bottles of Chianti, one with the woven grass skirt and one without. They were quickly delivered to the table.

Katie said, "Tony, you can't drink and drive and certainly not two bottles of wine. Rachel and Mike are too young to drink and I want to be awake for the concert."

"Easy there, mi amore. This is to show Rachel and Mike what real Chianti is all about. Not to drink it." Volpini was always the teacher, always reaching for the stars to stimulate the minds of his students.

Mike said, "That's cool, Mr. V."

Volpini continued, holding one of the bottles up, "The dried straw skirt on this one is called a fiasco. Chianti used to be sold only this way, a kind of trademark. Wine aficionados would often look down on Chianti as a bottom of the barrel wine so to speak, not worthy of comparison with, say, French Bordeaux wines. Chianti's were fiascos, they said. Some were and still are, but others are premier world class wines. You have to learn which is which."

Rachel asked, "So if they have the straw baskets, they're OK wines?"

"The skirt doesn't matter. Most Chianti's no longer have the skirt. Like this other bottle."

Volpini paused to look at the bottle without the skirt then continued, "The rules are complex but Chianti's are a mix of red and white grapes. By Italian law, a Chianti must have at least eighty percent red Sangiovese grapes. Then there's the Riserva which is kept in the barrel for at least thirty eight months and the Superiore which has higher alcohol content and other restrictions. Chianti is actually a geographic area divided into seven sub-areas." Rachel noticed that Volpini was flushed with the excitement of describing his favorite wines.

She said, "I'm impressed. Which is your favorite and what're you going to do with these two bottles?"

Mr. Volpini winked at Katie and said, "Let's put these in the trunk of the car unopened. Save them for a future occasion." Katie smiled wickedly. Then he said, "I like them all Rachel."

After dinner was ordered, Mr. Volpini invited the restaurant's regular singer over to the table and introduced everyone around. "We'd love to hear you sing *Torna a Sorriento,* Emilio."

"My pleasure, my friend."

Emilio walked over to the piano, spoke with the pianist and cleared his throat. Mr. V said, "Rachel, have you brought Mike up to date on your adventures with the police this week?"

Rachel, wanting Mike to concentrate on the upcoming song, simply said, "Adam and I are working on a drug case. I'll fill you in on the way home tonight."

Suddenly, Emilio's voice filled the room and the plaintive sounds of that haunting melody reached out to each diner. Rachel was transported to a far off village in Italy. Mike reacted differently than Rachel expected.

He reached over and touched Rachel on the arm. "I really like this place, Rach. I'm glad we're here." Rachel smiled and squeezed Mike's hand. Katie winked at Tony and the pianist leaned forward into her work. Mr. Volpini commented on the original Santa Lucía, saying she was born in Syracuse, Italy, and was the subject of an annual feast on December 13, still celebrated in Italy, but now mostly in Sweden.

The Italian food and song were over way too soon for Rachel.

Mr. V zipped through traffic to the U2 concert, arriving right on time.

What can you say about the energy Bono puts into a concert? He holds nothing back. The music soars and fulfills. The audience enthusiastically sang and clapped to *Where the Streets Have No Name* from the Joshua Tree album, arguably U2's best, and *Pride (In the Name of Love)* from the Unforgettable Fire, celebrating goodness in the face of evil, with Edge's guitar pushing Bono's voice to new heights. The audience was totally quiet for *With or Without You* in which you could almost hear the sound of a breaking heart. But all good things come to an end and after two encores this concert ended, too.

As they climbed back into Mr. V's car afterward, Rachel said, "Wasn't that fabulous? I've been in love with Bono for years. I've thought about going to Trinity College, Dublin to do a double major in science and Bono. And be closer to where he lives. Maybe I could see him on walks."

Mike, feeling a little jealous about the competition for Rachel's affections at this point, said, "Yeah, I like him, too. But he IS full of himself. My family lived in San Francisco when I was little, and I remember my Dad – a big U2 fan – telling the story about Bono doing a free concert downtown at the Embarcadero. Afterward he spray painted the statues in the water fountain black. Diane Feinstein was acting mayor. She said Bono would never do another concert in San Francisco while she was mayor. As far as I know, he hasn't."

From the front seat, Volpini said, as he inched out of the crowded parking lot, "Yeah, Feinstein became mayor because Dan White killed Harvey Milk, San Francisco's first openly gay mayor. Then there was the drama of White's trial. That trial became the first time the 'Twinkie Defense' was used in a murder case. The Dan White defense team argued that White shot Milk while high on sugar from eating too many Twinkies."

Katie said, "I'd forgotten about that sad episode in American jurisprudence. All Twinkies have ever done for me is increase my waistline."

In the back seat, Rachel pressed her thigh into Mike's. Then she said, "The reason I like Bono so much is that he is still married to his first wife and they have three great kids."

Mike, missing the point that monogamy gets Rachel's highest marks, but wanting to impress Rachel, said, "Bono was hired by Larry Moulin, the U2 founder, to be business manager. Bono was so aggressive he ended up being the lead singer. Tight!" He pressed back on Rachel's thigh and winked at her as if to say, 'Hey, I know something about Bono, too.'

As they passed San Juan Capistrano, Mike leaned over and kissed Rachel on the lips. His left hand brushed her breast. Was that an accident? Rachel thought. She responded by thrusting her tongue between Mike's slightly parted lips. Volpini noticed this development in the rear view mirror. He tapped Katie on the arm and in his fiercest growl bellowed, "All right back there!"

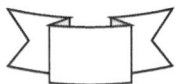

Chapter Eleven
The Plot Thickens
Monday, June 9

Adam pulled into the driveway at 6:30 PM Monday evening, an hour later than expected. The traffic at the San Ysidro border crossing into the U.S. had been so bad that it took forever to get through. Adam's stop for a margarita at the bar in Rosarita contributed to the delay. Mrs. Fuller was just serving the table when Adam walked in.

"Adam, so how did it go?" she asked.

"Sweet, Mom! Mr. Montenegro has helped me get off to a good start. You know, he's one smart manager," Adam responded.

Mrs. Fuller who had known the Montenegros for years said, "He's the best. And now you know Christina from our trip. She's a hoot, too." An unbidden image of Christina's chest popped into Adam's mind.

Mr. Fuller walked in from the living room. "Did you get to drive a truck today, Adam?"

"You bet. The truck depot is, like, way out. Mr. Delgado asked me to take a pickup truck from the depot to pick up a driver in Ensenada. Delgado's a take charge guy. There's no fooling around with him."

"Sounds like they're doing even better than I thought," said Mr. Fuller.

"Twenty seven trailers of produce were shipped all over México and to southern California today, a record," Adam reported.

After dinner, Rachel and Adam brought their parents up to speed on the identification of the white powder that Adam had found in the Cuyamaca Restaurant parking lot. Rachel had pushed Adam to come clean.

Mr. Fuller said, "Adam, why didn't you tell us about the powder?"

"I thought it might be baby powder, or something harmless, and wanted to check it out before I bothered you."

"Adam, do you think that scar faced guy dropped it?"

"Maybe it was that dude we saw him with, the one wearing the Mountain High School jacket," Adam said.

Mrs. Fuller said, "Adam, you and Rachel let the police handle this one. Don't lead the chase on solving a drug mystery."

Adam and Rachel exchanged a glance. They'd been involved in many adventures. Mrs. Fuller had not approved any of them. After they were over, she switched to being very proud of her two sleuths and glad that they had persisted in the chase.

Mrs. Fuller looked incredulous. "I feel like I've just come into the middle of the conversation. Will someone please explain to me we what's going on here?"

Mr. Fuller sounded a little defensive. "Adam and I bumped into a pair of characters at the Cuyamaca Restaurant two Saturdays ago. One of them hit the Jag when he left. Adam thought he and Rachel had seen one of them while they were sailing."

Mrs. Fuller said, "Rachel, don't you even think of going to México with Adam on this one. And Rachel you need to hit the books tonight for a change."

To lift the conversation, Rachel responded, "Prayers are still conducted at San Diego public schools, have you heard?"

Mr. Fuller said, "Against the law, I believe, Rachel."

"Mr. V said today that as long as there are tests, there will be prayers in school."

That brought a chuckle and broke the tension over white

powders and bad men.

While Rachel told her little joke, Adam was thinking it would not be a good time to tell his parents any more about his job.

So Adam simply said, "Mom, you worry too much."

Mrs. Fuller knew that Adam was right but felt her uneasiness increase anyway.

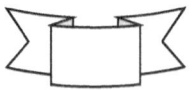

Chapter Twelve

Corvette

Saturday, June 14

Mr. Volpini's garage in Tierrasanta hid a black 1967 427-435 Chevrolet Corvette. Volpini was restoring it. Adam stood in the garage admiring the progress. Mr. V bought the car because he liked the 427 cubic inch motor with 435 horsepower, known as the L71 engine option, the most powerful engine available in a 1960's production automobile. Mr. V's car was built in the last year before Federal smog laws reduced engine power with mandated emissions equipment. The Positraction 4.11 rear end minimized slip of the rear tires by applying power to the tire with the best traction, a new option on production cars at the time.

This was Mr. V's first restoration. His first try at restoration ended in mononucleosis before he started. On his sixteenth birthday in Italy, his parents had agreed he could begin his dream project on an old Fiat he was about to buy. Then he was down for six weeks with swollen glands and before he could find another suitable car, the family decided to move to the States.

The Corvette had been stored in a garage for twenty years when Volpini found it, the owner just deceased. At the time, the car wasn't running, had cracks in the dust-covered fiberglass body and windshield, and sported four flat tires. Mr. V fell in love with the car and bought it on the spot from the deceased owner's sister. That same afternoon he towed the car home on a flatbed truck.

Adam kept an old flea market calendar on his bedroom wall showing a red Corvette convertible. A dark haired model leaned back on the front fender. Adam liked Corvettes. This admiration in no way diminished his love for the Alfa Romeo Spyder that he and Rachel used as a daily school commuter and weekend freedom wagon for his senior year.

When Rachel first heard about the Corvette she said to Adam, "Mr. V drives a Ford Thunderbird and he buys a General Motors Corvette? He's schizophrenic."

Adam had laughed and said when Mr. V wised up he'd probably trade them both in on a Chrysler Jeep.

Today, the Corvette was up on the AutoPro 6000 hydraulic lift Mr. V had installed in the second bay of his garage, every car buff's dream. No more hand jacks and jack stands which are both slippery and dangerous.

The first job Mr. V tackled when he had the AutoPro was removing the 427 engine and taking it to a Chevrolet speed shop for disassembly and rebuilding. New pistons, rings, tappets, bearings and seals were included in the job. All moving parts were balanced. The block was repainted red-orange to look like new. The valve covers were polished. The finished engine was set up on a dynamometer to see whether everything worked, whether there were fluid leaks, and to test the horsepower: 437 BHP at 5500 RPM. Better than new. And no leaks.

The original aluminum wheels were shipped out of town for complete restoration. One new wheel was required as the old one was badly bent. The suspension parts were disassembled and powder coated in black at a local shop. The result of powder coating old metal parts is a hard, shiny surface that looks like new, but lasts far longer under use than regular enamel paint. Front and rear suspension bushings had been replaced with New Old Stock (NOS) parts, hard to find but important in a serious car restoration, and reassembled. Some of Mr. V's students had helped with various tasks. But not Adam. Adam liked driving cars and thinking about them. Wrenches were just not his thing.

The last step taken by Mr. V was buying five new Goodyear 775/15 Power Cushion GPC4 tires, the original style Corvette tires now available from Lucas Tires in Los Angeles. Lucas was where the Fullers found new original style Pirelli Cinturatos for the Alfa Spyder when they needed authentic tires to match the character of the car.

Then Mr. V then hit the wall, so to speak. Overwhelmed by the hundreds of small tasks in a restoration, Mr. V stopped work for nearly two years. Cash flow had also been a factor. But three months ago he'd mustered his enthusiasm and started again. He had the rolling chassis, sans engine, towed to Tijuana where a body shop he trusted with special expertise in fiberglass restored the body and paint work inside and out. With twenty four coats of hand-rubbed black lacquer paint, this car now looked better than new. New reproduction rubber moldings were installed around the doors and trunk lid, replacing the original rubber pieces. And the price in Tijuana had been less than half the quotes he'd received in San Diego. The car looked like a million dollars when it returned from Tijuana.

But the big news with a Corvette from the sixties is what happens when the engine is started. Adam loved the sound on the rare occasions he'd heard one. The big Corvette engines would pound you in the gut with excitement while assaulting your ear drums with bass music.

Years earlier, Adam watched Dustin Hoffman's performance in *The Graduate* at home with the family eating popcorn and drinking Cokes. In one scene, Hoffman drives the red 1967 Alfa Romeo Duetto Spyder. When Mr. Fuller heard the sound of the engine, he leaped right out of his chair, shouting, 'Fake!' The movie producer dubbed the sound track with a V-8 engine, leaving the beautiful sound of the high revving Italian four cylinder engine on the cutting room floor. V-8's *rumbled* better than four cylinder engines, four cylinder engines *screamed* better than V-8's, but Mr. Fuller was incredulous at discovering this assault on automotive historical accuracy. He claimed even the popcorn didn't taste the same afterward.

Standing in Mr. V's garage, Adam smiled at the recollection. Adam felt it all depended on what mood you were in as to which engine you liked better.

Adam planned to be around the garage when Mr. V finally mated the restored engine to the four speed transmission, put it in the car and drove the car out of the garage for the first time. This would not happen today, though, and probably not for quite a while, Adam mused to himself. Mr. V had just finished installing the new braided steel brake lines and asked for Adam's help in bleeding the brakes.

"So tell me, Adam, how did you come out on the AP physics exam?"

Adam said, "One thing at a time, Mr. V.   Let's bleed the brakes first then talk physics."

The AutoPro was lowered to ground position and Adam inserted in the driver's seat. Then the AutoPro was raised part way. Now Mr. V could add the Castrol LMA silicone brake fluid to the renovated brake system and still get underneath the car to bleed the brakes. Mr. V used modern seals and brake fluids, not authentic, but good for safety and availability reasons. Some professional restoration shops would use only original materials and fluids.   Volpini insisted on one hundred percent authenticity, except in the cases of unusually high expense or safety.   The latest silicone brake fluid could take higher heat and did not absorb water like earlier brake fluids.

Volpini also insisted on maintaining matching serial numbers on the engine and transmission. They had to be the units installed at the factory which made them correct for the serial number of the car. Experts pointed out that it might be cheaper to buy an already rebuilt engine and transmission instead of overhauling the ones that were original to the car but Volpini wouldn't cave in on that point.

Mr. V'd also found New Old Stock metallic brake pads, which squeaked when cold, took a long time to heat up properly, but never faded under heavy use. Corvette added four wheel disk brakes to the cars from 1965 on, so this car sported disc brakes. Mr. V aspired to race slalom courses for Sports Car Club of America Solo II events and wanted the brakes to be the best possible. They were.

"OK, Adam, hold the brake pedal down. Atta boy! Up. Hold. Down. Hold. Up. Hold. Down. Hold. Adam, I'm going to make a mechanic out of you yet!" They soon finished the brakes.

"How about a refreshing drink now that training is over, Adam?"

"Good idea. To answer your earlier question, Mr. V, I got a five on the AP Physics exam. No sweat."

"Any surprises on it?" Volpini expected a five.

"Not really." Adam never revealed more than the necessary minimum. "But I'd like to bring you up to date on what Rachel and I've found out in México. Can you believe I've been working there almost two weeks already?" They washed up with pink hand cleaner paste that Mr. V kept by the sink in the garage and walked into his kitchen. Adam thought the kitchen was exceptionally clean and neat for a bachelor like Mr. V.

Adam reviewed the evidence with Mr. Volpini that he and Rachel had gathered so far on the drug gang.

"Rachel's hunch is that the Julian incident is related to Méxican-American and that I'm in the middle of this and don't even know it yet." Adam concluded.

"Whoa, Adam! You're going too fast for me. Remember, I'm a science teacher. I need to take things a step at a time. How can I help?"

"What's our next step in gathering evidence? So far, we've got what Rachel and I guess is going on. We barely understand that. We do have proof that the white powder is cocaine. We can try to match this first sample to any future batches we find. The rest is circumstantial."

"Here's an idea, Adam. Let me give you a fingerprint kit. I get these from my DEA drug enforcement buddies. Use the kit to dust the inside of the electronics box you're installing on the trucks when the trucks come back in. If one is tampered with, you might just catch the person who did it by getting his prints. Keep your eyes peeled for evidence of cocaine, meth or heroin on the truck frames or in odd places. You know what the powders look like from that book I showed you. If the trucks are being used for taking the drugs north, you may find a powder. Use a scraper and your supply of Ziploc bags. We'll ask Jake Steinberg to send a detective down to bring anything you find back so you don't get caught at the border." Mr. V suggested other ideas like hiring handlers with drug sniffing dogs for random inspections.

"Could I pick up that kit after graduation this afternoon?"

"Sure, see me at the dessert table and we'll walk over to my room and get you one." The Seaside High School graduation was catered every year by the school's kitchen staff and Mr. V had a reputation for hanging out at the dessert table. For seniors, having their photos taken with this favored science teacher while he devoured a favored dessert was too good an opportunity to pass up.

Mr. V continued. "Adam, you planning to pull your pants up for the graduation ceremony?"

The height at which Adam wore his pants was a joke between them now, but early in Adam's high school career, Adam earned demerits for wearing regulation Sue Mills pants so low his underwear showed. Adam's shoes were often untied, too, but it wasn't clear whether he did these violations of the dress code on purpose or was just tuned out.

"Yeah, sure Mr. V. With the graduation robes you couldn't tell anyway. I've been thinking about going barefoot, though. Everyone could see that." Adam was on thin ice with his parents, too, about lack of attention to what he wore, so he would probably not go barefoot today. But Volpini didn't know that.

"OK, then, just in case I'll have my camera ready to gather the evidence. Then I'll let the administration deal with you. You've been at this school for twelve years, Adam. I'm finished with trying to straighten you out." Mr. V put a lot of energy into scorching Adam.

"Can't believe you're letting me win, Mr. V. See you at graduation at two!"

Graduation was a dignified event but featured the inevitable screw-ups. The high school band got lost once on the processional Pomp and Circumstance and had to start over. The band teacher almost had a heart attack. Chris Demarais tripped on the first step of the bleachers and crashed into Tina Denton. They both fell down. Sue Mondavi took her cap off to fluff her hair and dropped the cap between the bleacher steps. One of the boys was able to reach down and grab it, but a ripple of nervous laughter went through the senior class. They were ready to sit down with a command from the headmaster.

Students on the high risers strained to see their out of town relatives in the audience seats and talked out of the corners of their mouths to anyone within earshot. On the signal, everyone sat down except one of the boys on the back row who hadn't been paying attention. Two other boys grabbed him and pulled him down. Rachel, sitting in the audience, saw with relief that Adam was doing everything right for a change.

The graduation speaker, a Seaside High School parent from Croatia, spoke about immigrants who had succeeded in America, an inspiring thirty minute talk. When valedictorian Sue Shane's peppy, funny talk ended, the headmaster called for the tassels to be moved to the other side of the caps. Then the class recessed from the stands without further incident. As they came down the aisle, as one the entire class took their caps off and pitched them high in the air.

Julie, greeted Adam in the sea of graduates afterwards and said, "Congratulations! You looked great up there." She hesitated. "Adam, Rachel just filled me in on your adventures in México. I want to go with you to Ensenada on Monday now that I know what you're up to. And go for a ride in one of your trucks."

"Let me get organized first. Then you can join me for a day. Just make sure your parents give you the green light when the time comes. I don't want any trouble with them."

"You've been telling everyone how safe it is. Right? They should be OK with me going for just one day."

"I'm helping Méxican-American add electronics to trucks which is as safe as a summer job can be. Let's wait a week or so and we'll do it. But now, let's party!" Adam laughed, grabbed Julie and swept her up into the air.

Several of Adam's classmates caught Adam for a 'seniors only sailing team photo.' The cameras flashed again. Then the happy crowd started to thin out as the graduates went home to change for the all-night party in the Field House.

Adam spotted Mr. V. The two immediately went to Volpini's lab where Adam picked up the fingerprint kit. He left Mr. V, found

Julie and dropped her off at her house to change for the post-grad party. Adam couldn't wait to see Julie's jungle outfit which she promised he would never forget.

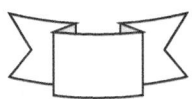

Chapter Thirteen

Survivor Night

Saturday, June 14

When Adam picked her up at her house at six o'clock, Julie was wearing an ankle length rain coat, fancy high heels and formal makeup. She looked like she was ready for a New York City night club. Adam surprised Julie by showing up in a leopard skin outfit and bare feet. But Adam was forced to hide his disappointment when he saw Julie's costume.

When they arrived back on campus, Adam couldn't hold off making a comment any longer. As they got out of the car, he said,

"Hey, you look beautiful tonight. Your outfit is cool but I expected something different."

"You wait. The night has just begun."

The theme of the party was from the hit TV show "Survivor," complete with jungles, swamps and eight inch long plastic "bugs." The conversational buzz was how well the decorations committee had made this event realistic.

Intrigued, Adam took Julie by the arm and they walked up to the Field House door. The admission process inside proceeded under the eyes of two parent volunteers who were both eating and offering real chocolate covered fried ants. Adam and Julie tried the fried ants.

Through a mouthful Adam said to Julie, "These aren't half bad." She grimaced but swallowed some, too. During the inspection of outfits for conformance to the rules, Julie lived up to Adam's highest expectation. She opened her raincoat to reveal a spectacular hot pink bathing suit with large green polka dots. Julie took off her high heels, rolled her raincoat around them and turned them in for safe keeping in the storage area behind the registration table.

The idea of a mud party for Survivor Night had its origins a few years earlier in a group of Seaside parents who moved from Westland, Michigan to San Diego. They'd become big financial contributors to Seaside so had stroke with the administration. Mud Day had been a successful annual event in Westland that kids loved. The Seaside Board of Directors had been consulted by the Administration to see if a modified Mud Day would work at Seaside and had given approval with certain restrictions: heavy chaperoning, short hours and professional preparation of the mud.

A San Diego pool firm was hired to provide ninety tons of

sanitized mud and ten thousand gallons of chlorinated water, just half the size of the Westland mud pool. The first year success of this event propelled the second mud party forward, now the centerpiece of Survivor Night. Jungle plants surrounded the mud pool for realism.

Another inspiration for the Seaside mud party is held annually at a Brazilian colonial seaside town, Paraty. This one erupts each year during Carnival craze -- a parade in which the only costume required is layers of thick, dark, sticky mud. Seaside didn't go this far, but the parade idea stuck, so to speak, and became part of Survivor Night. Paraty uses a blue-black mud which the indigenous Indians had used for ages for medicinal purposes. Seaside mud made no medicinal claims.

The first event after eating the chocolate ants was the Swamp Scamper in which each couple waded through the swamp, an artificial mess created by deranged parents in the rented above-ground swimming pool measuring fifty feet long and thirty feet wide. The result was knee deep water, mud and even large-leafed plants. After the Scamper, wet mud covered Adam and Julie from head to toe.

Julie's stunning hot pink bathing suit with polka dots turned dark brown. Adam's leopard spots were gone, too, hidden under mud.

There was a similarity between Survivor Night and the 'Survivor' TV show. A vote by each couple after each event was taken by parents with clip boards. The goal was to recognize outstanding effort in the games, but in effect couples were voted out of the running by not getting votes. Votes were tallied for a grand prize to be awarded at the end of the games.

The next game was the Race for Cash, one partner running the length of the mud pool, tagging the waiting partner who then ran back. This was done in groups of six couples, so mud flew. There were cash prizes from the Student Council party fund of twenty five dollars for the winning couple in each heat.

The main event, six-man Mud Volleyball, was the most popular. Imagine jumping to spike the ball and having the mud suck your feet into no jump at all. Smearing the ball with extra mud before each serve was popular. Goggles were mandatory. The games were to twelve points, speed scoring, and sudden death. The games were fast, the whistles loose and soon a winner was crowned. Mud-covered volleyballs were worn by the winners as hats on a parade lap around the pool. Supported by both hands.

"You look muddy, Julie," Adam noted at one point, looking her over from top to bottom.

"I look a lot like you do, brownie," she responded, laughing. "Good thing the Field House has been heated to eighty degrees or I'd never make it."

"No question we'd both have pneumonia by now if this were outside," Adam responded. "What do you say we enter the Mud Wrestling Contest?"

Julie winked and squeezed Adam's hand in response.

The Mud Wrestling Contest took place in a roped off corner of the main pool. The Administration had insisted that boys wrestled boys and girls wrestled girls. You had thirty seconds to pin your opponent, no exceptions. A lost bathing suit or part thereof was automatic forfeiture for both wrestlers.

Adam was quickly eliminated by George "The Cave" Cavenopolis, heavyweight captain of the Seaside wrestling team, and Julie was pinned by The Cave's date, Sandy Jameson, in nothing flat. Sandy had pumped a lot of iron by the tender age of eighteen and dispatched Julie almost as fast as The Cave got Adam.

Adam and Julie won the "Best Messed" award at the 3 AM

break. The Best Messed contest helped the chaperones stay in charge. And it helped the participants stay up all night. Each couple walked by the judges, arm in arm, stopping, turning then walking off the raised stage. Winners were then brought back to the podium for medals. One couple dozed off during the contest while leaning against the wall. The DJ turned up the volume on the next CD, and everyone stood in a circle around them clapping until they awoke, embarrassed at being the only ones to succumb to sleep up to that point.

For their Best Messed trophy, Adam and Julie both received a bamboo cup engraved with the Seaside High logo and "Best Messed." Their picture was taken by the school photographer who, although fully dressed, was also covered in mud. As they posed for the photo, Adam and Julie were all bright white teeth on a brown mud background.

After coming off the podium with their trophies, Julie said, "Adam, this is the best night ever for me. I've loved every minute."

Adam grabbed her and gave her a big kiss on her mud crusted mouth to a 'Woot, woot!' from the crowd. Then he said, "You're such a gem, Julie. What'll I ever do without you?"

"Adam, when you're away at Dartmouth, I'll be your long forgotten high school honey."

"We have email, Skype and Christmas, Babe," Adam grinned. "I want you to come for Fall and Spring Weekends. Takes less than a week to get to Dartmouth from here." Julie smiled at this. "Besides, I like the idea of a high school honey. You'll keep me in the library on weekends. Keep me from flunking out my first semester."

"I'll bet you'll find a way to escape the library," Julie said, faking a good pout.

As Adam dropped Julie off at her house at 6 AM Sunday, Julie said, "Adam, I want you to be careful this week in Mexico. Call me." They kissed good morning and Adam drove home smiling. Oddly, Sonia came into his mind as he pulled into the Fuller driveway and realized that she was asleep in the guest room.

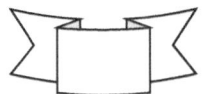

Chapter Fourteen

Sophomore-Junior Prom

Saturday, June 14

In order to attend the Sophomore-Junior Prom, Rachel had to escape her grounding for a week after messing up big time the night of the Bono concert. Kira was to arrange Prom Committee approval for her cousin Alex Sampson and his date Sonia Vidaña as special guests.

After the Bono concert, Rachel and Mike had gotten out of Volpini's Thunderbird and thanked Katie and Tony profusely for the wonderful evening. Then Rachel went into the house, observed that all the lights were out and everyone was asleep. She waited inside until

Mr. V left. Mike waited in his car. It was 2 AM.

Rachel then stepped back outside and closed the front door very quietly. She jumped into Mike's car, he started the engine and they headed for the overlook at Sunset Cliffs. Three hours at the overlook went by faster than Rachel expected. When the sun started to light the eastern sky, Rachel knew she was in big trouble. She was right on the money on that one, sweet potato. Her parents were outraged that she had stayed out all night without permission.

Considering everything, grounding for a week was actually mild punishment.

But Rachel devised a comeback plan. On Tuesday of graduation week, she'd cleaned her room without being asked and done the family laundry after school. On Wednesday, she'd announced an "A" in her history final, now graded, with a potential as a result for an A- in the course. This would give her a straight 'A' average for the semester, a good place to start her negotiation. On Thursday, she volunteered to get the family groceries, peeling the ever-present list off the refrigerator, and with a smile, joined her Mom for the weekly ritual. Normally, she would do anything to avoid going.

On Thursday night, Rachel moved her plan forward. She casually mentioned to Mr. and Mrs. Fuller that Mike had asked her out to the sophomore-junior post-graduation party on Saturday, and if they could somehow forgive her for her transgressions, she would be forever grateful to get a one-day-early release from her grounding which ended Sunday. After all, what was twenty four hours out of seven days if she was truly repentant and had served her time as a model daughter?

Anticipating this discussion, Mr. and Mrs. Fuller had prepared negotiating room. Mr. Fuller said, "Rachel, we're your biggest fans and we love you unconditionally. But what you did had to be punished. You do understand that?"

"Yes, Dad. I'm SO sorry. One of the reasons I'm asking for early release is that Sonia, Mr. Montenegro's administrative assistant, wants to come to the party with me. Adam is so impressed with Sonia that I called her to see if she'd be interested in a date with Kira's cousin, Alex Hampton. Kira asked if I would help her find someone for Alex. Sonia said yes, so I've invited her to stay with us in our guest room, if that's OK."

"Of course," Mr. Fuller said, "we'd be delighted to have her stay with us. But Rachel, the punishment was for seven days. We can't change that." Rachel looked crestfallen. "However, since you did so well on your finals, we'll give you a suspended sentence for Saturday with the punishment to resume Sunday and add Monday for a total of eight days."

Rachel jumped up, hugged her parents, and said, "Thanks SO much. You two are the greatest parents. I won't ever disappoint you like this again." She ran off down the hall to call Mike with the good news. Mr. Fuller winked at Mrs. Fuller who winked back.

Rachel's Sophomore-Junior Prom party was held at the Hilton on Mission Bay and proved to be a tad more elegant than the senior's Survivor Night party. For openers, this event was black tie.

The ground lights around the hotel lit up the walkways and the palm trees, adding atmosphere. Sonia Vidaña wore an exotic long black dress that complemented her black hair and black evening gloves. Alex and Sonia were seated with Mike and Rachel and another couple at a table near the dance floor.

Rachel signaled to Sonia and got her away from their table for a minute to talk.

"Rachel, I really like Alex. Thanks for arranging this. He's so funny. He told me when he was in high school he earned a gentleman's C in every course."

"Actually the opposite Sonia. He did well academically, but decided not to go to college for other reasons," Rachel said. Alex had graduated from high school six years earlier and now managed a boating supply store in Pt. Loma. Rachel and Adam saw him often when buying sailboat parts. Alex also raced motorcycles and had competed twice in the Baja 1000, the thousand mile off road race run annually in Baja California. Adam had long had his eye on trying that race but had absolutely no support from anyone at home for the idea.

"I thought you'd like Alex. According to Kira, he's the greatest dancer. Try to get him to do a salsa or meringue with you. The band will be playing those." Sonia glowed with anticipation.

"Where did you and Mike disappear to?" Rachel and Mike had been gone for an hour or so earlier.

"We walked along Mission Bay behind the hotel. Saw lots of stars." She winked at Sonia. The two had become fast friends in only a few hours. "Try it. But don't forget to come back. Next stop is the after party at Kira's house, from 2-4 AM. Then we make tracks home before Mike's car turns into a pumpkin and I get grounded for another week."

Sure enough, it was exactly 4:30 AM when Mike and Alex pulled up at the Fuller home with Rachel and Sonia. Rachel's goodnight kiss from Mike was intense since they knew it had to last at least until Tuesday. Rachel couldn't see what Alex and Sonia did.

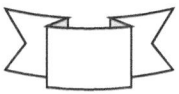

Chapter Fifteen
Engineering
Monday, June 16

Adam arrived for his third week of work in Ensenada bristling with energy after twelve hours in the rack recovering from Survivor Night. He was second into the office at 7:30 AM so the door was already unlocked.

Adam researched ideas for truck data acquisition, positioning and data communications systems all week leading up to Saturday's graduation. He also visited several San Diego area companies and completed an Internet search. Considering that Adam found time to pull three all-nighters at various year-end parties, he'd made the best of the last week of his high school career.

Adam started to write the report on his findings on the computer based on notes he'd made from his research.

At 7:45 AM, Sonia arrived and looked in on Adam working away. "Good morning, Adam. Got here early?"

"Hello again. Yep. Got lots of sleep last night and want to finish my report this morning. Nice dress, Sonia."

She blushed at the compliment. "It's new. I've been looking for a sleeveless black dress for work and I found this at Sanborn's in Tijuana. Coffee?"

"That'd be great, especially if you throw in a couple of cookies." He smiled at her and she disappeared.

At 8 AM, Mr. Montenegro arrived and stopped in to say good morning. "Adam, you're sure here bright and early. I'd like a progress report today."

"Fine Mr. Montenegro, I'll be ready before lunch. By the way, my Dad will call you about the new telescope. He's very pleased to hear you're interested in the project."

"Good. I look forward to that. You know, when I was at State he and I'd get together over coffee in the morning and talk about extraterrestrial life and car racing, things like that. We'd argue about the Frank Drake equation which predicts a thousand intelligent civilizations in the Milky Way galaxy. I still think that number is low. And his passion for cars is catchy. He invited me to go with him to the Laguna Seca raceway near San Francisco three years running." Montenegro's voice was nostalgic, evidence he missed those wild trips with Mr. Fuller.

"Yeah, Dad is car crazy and Frank Drake is one of my astronomy heroes, too. Still hard to prove his equation is wrong, though," Adam responded. "And it's only a matter of time before we find another intelligent civilization. Then we have to figure out how to get to them, or vice versa, given the distances."

"By the time we got there and back, all our friends would be dead, even if we travelled near the speed of light. Who'd want to go?"

Adam continued the idea. "Have you seen the Planetary Society work on light sails? Rockets propelled by the pressure of sunlight on a special aluminized sail. The rocket goes faster and faster until it runs out of sunlight around Jupiter's orbit. Then a sun-orbiting high powered laser system is trained on the sail which provides more concentrated light to push the rocket out of the solar system and off to the next star."

"No question that you're your father's son, Adam."

Sonia Vidaña brought in Mr. Montenegro's moustache cup filled with steaming coffee on a tray with Adam's. Adam was intrigued by Montenegro's coffee cup with the porcelain bar across the top that prevented a moustache from getting wet. Montenegro's moustache was as black as the coffee, a full handlebar no less. And it stayed dry as he sipped the coffee.

"Fine then, Adam, let's plan on 11 AM in my office." He left.

Adam said, "All right Sonia, where are the rest of my cookies?" Sonia laughed.

"By the way," Adam continued, "Rachel said you were an out

of sight hit at the Sophomore-Junior party. Sorry I missed you all weekend, but the seniors go off and do their own thing."

"I had a wonderful time. Rachel and your parents made all the arrangements and your guest room is perfect. I came back early yesterday for a family get together. I left your house before you even showed up for breakfast. Alex was so much fun. We danced the salsa all night! And be sure to thank your parents for so graciously taking care of me."

Adam stopped for a second, looking at Sonia. What is it about this woman, he thought to himself. Then aloud, "Sure will. By the way, glad Alex worked out. I have to admit he was Rachel's idea. Got to get to work now." Was that a blush he saw on Sonia's face?

Adam presented his findings in Mr. Montenegro's office at 11 AM sharp. Pictures of various generations of the company's trucks and drivers were arranged on the walls of Montenegro's office. Adam noted that Félix Delgado was the driver of one rig then scanned the others to see where Delgado appeared again. He was in a number of them.

Adam said, "Mr. Delgado is in a lot of those photos like the one of him working under the hood of that old Ford F-150 pickup." The blue pickup truck looked tired and beat up in a photo that must have been taken sixteen years earlier. Adam had instantly liked the slender, black haired manager of operations. Félix had been helpful to Adam already, explaining the complexities of operating a fifty two tractor, ninety trailer fleet in two countries.

"That old Ford was our first truck. We kept it running for years after we had outgrown it and didn't really need it anymore. We were very sentimental about that truck. And I'm sentimental about Félix, too. He's one of the main reasons for the company's success. He's held every job and done every one well. But now, Adam, to your report."

"Mr. Montenegro, the key to making your trucks safe from outsiders is to add new information technology to each truck. Your trucks must be fitted with sensitive detectors and location systems plus the communications capability to send data back to the depot south of town and directly to your office here. That way, we'll have data redundancy and instant updates. If one of the two links is down, the other serves. You'll be able to watch the trucks in real time with onboard video cameras. I'd like the communication link to your office to be our secret. For security." Adam showed Mr. Montenegro the report he'd just finished which included color sketches Rachel had made for him showing where the equipment would be located on a typical truck. Rachel had a knack for drawing full perspective sketches of mechanical systems. Or almost anything else for that matter. Her truck sketches looked like trucks.

"Adam, I'm impressed, but what's all this going to cost us? Looks expensive to me. Our customers won't hold still for price increases to pay for technology."

"Maybe they will. Hear me out. The upfront cost per truck is small compared with the price of a new truck or the cost of getting caught carrying drugs. Microprocessors and cameras are cheap these days and getting less expensive all the time. Moore's Law says that the number of transistor chips on a substrate doubles every two years. This means everything gets smaller and costs less all the time."

"Right. If I remember, that's been true since 1958."

Adam continued to explain that the communications links are a bit up there in price, but worth it to catch the bad guys in real time. As backup, the data is dumped at the end of each roundtrip run back at the truck depot. Programs will be written to analyze the daily data to see trends and variations as they develop. Data would include where each truck stops, date and time for each event monitored, miles between stops, with sniffers to sample, detect and record the presence of foreign substances like marijuana or methamphetamine. Video would record images and sounds anytime a truck is stopped. The accuracy of the Global Positioning System would yield truck location within one hundred feet or less at all times.

"Adam, I can see where you're going with this and like it. History files on each truck's route and timing, so if a truck stops to take on drugs, you'll know where and when. The sniffers would tell you what the drug is. The demand for different drugs is changing. The Méxican Army just found and captured fifteen tons of methamphetamines in one raid. Street value as much as $7.5 billion. Meth wasn't a major factor in México a decade ago. So I like the flexibility of adding new drugs."

"Over time we'll be able to detect them all," Adam interjected.

Montenegro rose from his seat and walked over to the window which looked out over Ensenada. He said, "Part of our success will be in hiding the onboard systems, letting only a few key employees know what we're doing." Montenegro was headed for giving the green light, Adam could tell.

A pause in the conversation let them both savor the potential for what they were about to do.

Montenegro continued, "Adam, this will work. I'd like to start installation on the first truck as soon as we can get the parts together."

Montenegro then explained that he'd have the work done at Radios Impresivos in Tijuana, since they were already doing a Blue

Tooth hands free cellular upgrade on the tractors. He explained that it should be easier to keep it quiet there than in Ensenada, that the owner of Radios Impresivos, Jorge Salmón, is a close friend and can be trusted to be discreet.

"I'll meet Delgado later today to discuss the program. He'll know what we're up to but no one else. One additional subterfuge I'm going to try is that only you and I will know that the first truck has the secret communications link to my office."

"Good plan, Mr. Montenegro. I'm certain these systems will stop funny business on your trucks. I'd like to ride along with the first truck we convert. Rachel is interested in joining me. After all, she drew the pictures in my report."

"OK," Montenegro said, turning to the shipping schedule on his wall. "Let's see when we can arrange it. If we finish converting the first truck next Monday, we have …. Let's see…a load of peppers going from Compañias Ferrér in San Quintín to the market in Mexicali on Wednesday. The new Ford 750 tractors have three abreast seating in the cab, so you two could easily make that run along with the regular driver."

"Cool," Adam said. "I know this is the right move."

"Now let's get a bite to eat. It's already 1:30PM! Two and a half hours have flown past. Let's grab tacos on one of the stands around the corner. If you haven't had Ensenada tacos, you haven't eaten a taco. The handmade salsa, avocado, sour cream and onions are the best. Then let's stop in to see Sr. Salmón on our way through Tijuana and get the truck conversions launched."

Adam's mouth was watering for an Ensenada taco.

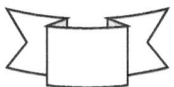

Chapter Sixteen

To Mexicali

Wednesday, June 24

Adam and Rachel arrived at Méxican-American's truck depot south of Ensenada at 6 AM Wednesday morning. Road trip!

Rachel, final exams behind her and with an A- in history felt like a bird escaped from a cage. Her grounding ended yesterday. She was officially a junior. Now she was looking for adventure and was about to find it. Rachel had decided to tell her parents she would be at school today, getting ready for a summer art class. How would they find out that she had detoured to Ensenada? Adam was having a hard time figuring why Rachel wanted to practice this deception on their parents.

"Mom is still worried about you working in México this summer. Her intuition, she says. I just don't want to add fuel to the fire by including me in her worries," Rachel had argued.

"OK with me Rach but I think they'll find out anyway," Adam had said.

The big red diesel tractor was idling at the truck depot south of Ensenada, ready for the run south part way toward San Quintín, there to hook up with a trailer loaded with red, green and yellow peppers for delivery in Mexicali.

Rachel said, "Adam, this depot is big. I've never seen anything like it. How many trucks are kept here?"

"All of the fifty two tractors plus ninety trailers and smaller trucks owned by Méxican-American are based here. But their job is to be on the road earning money. So at any one time, you'll see ten or fifteen trucks and a few trailers here. The rest are all over Baja California and the southwestern U. S. Some of our ninety trailers" – Adam, as an employee of Méxican-American, had already taken ownership of the trucks – "are left at customer sites for loading and unloading, without tying up an expensive tractor until the tractor is needed."

Rachel had this image in her head of tractors being big, green vehicles with "John Deere" written on the side. They should also have big rubber-ridged driving wheels and small steering wheels up front. She found it funny that truck tractors and farm tractors were so totally different.

The driver, Jorge Camarena, walked up. "Hello, Adam. Are you ready?"

"Yes, Jorge. This is my sister, Rachel. She's joining us today. Plenty of room for all of us." Jorge nodded his agreement with the plan.

Camarena said, "Mr. Delgado gave me the heads up about Rachel going along. Good to meet you Rachel," he said, a big smile on his face. Jorge's expression said that he was going to enjoy a truck ride with this attractive American girl. He turned to Adam, "Right. We're taking the new F-750 tractor, the first to get the electronics package. Arrived back from Tijuana yesterday afternoon. Guillermo drove it down. Get ready. We leave in ten minutes."

"What's wrong with him?" Rachel said as Jorge disappeared inside the office.

"Rach he likes you. He'll get over having another passenger."

Adam noticed through the window that Jorge was on the telephone. He wondered if Jorge was updating Compañias Ferrér on their arrival time. But there was something about Jorge's manner, maybe the way he looked over his shoulder at the siblings that bothered Adam. Adam ran inside to the men's room, passing close by Jorge. Occupied. Adam was about to burst and remembered how long a minute is depends on which side of the bathroom door you're on. Afterward, Adam and Jorge ended up returning to the rig together.

The three left the parking lot in the new tractor headed south to the farm where the loaded trailer awaited.

Rachel said she had a joke to tell. "I once went to a Méxican restaurant in San Diego. The waiter poured a glass of water then warned me not to drink it."

Adam laughed, but Rachel couldn't stop laughing, which made Adam laugh even more. They fed on each other. Jorge didn't even smile.

Rachel then told a story about a Méxican restaurant with Chinese waiters, but that joke didn't go anywhere.

As they traveled south, Adam pointed to the burned out car at the bottom of a cliff. The trio stopped for coffee at the Café del Sol. Rachel bought cookies for the trip. They'd eat lunch in Mexicali at one of the one hundred and fifty or so Chinese restaurants that populated that city. Rachel pointed out they'd most likely employ Méxican waiters.

Later Jorge said as they turned into the Compañias Ferrér driveway, "We'll be leaving for Mexicali right away. The load will be heavy so we'll not get to Mexicali until before noon. There're ten thousand curves on the route between Ensenada and Mexicali but it's a pretty drive. Couple of hours to switch trailers and eat and we'll be back in Ensenada by 4 PM. We'll make better time empty on the return trip."

Compañias Ferrér in the early morning light looked to Adam like it had on his first visit two weeks earlier – a dusty, quaint operation sitting quietly without too much apparent forward motion. But Adam enjoyed the solitude of the early morning no matter where he was. Here the steady unbroken quiet was pleasant, the smells of this farming community increasing as the sun reached the volatile organic materials that were so abundant. Adam recalled out loud that one of the characteristics of organic substances is low boiling points – hence volatility and the odors all around them.

Rachel responded, "Wow, the esters are everywhere," echoing Adam's words.

By 8:10 AM the tractor was hooked to the trailer on the Compañias Ferrér produce dock. The load consisted of eight tons of peppers, a big load, but everything was right on schedule.

Heading back north along the route just traveled, Jorge said, "You guys just relax and leave the driving to me. I know this road like the back of my hand." Rachel and Adam chitchatted about Mike and Rachel's plan to visit the Campo railway museum the coming weekend. Mike loved model trains and wanted Rachel to learn to share this enthusiasm. Adam told Rachel the story about the kidnapping of José Ferrér at the main stoplight in San Quintín. That quieted Rachel down. She sat watching the countryside go by.

In Ensenada, the gleaming truck turned north east on Route 3, the main road to Mexicali.

Adam asked, "Think the traffic will be heavy?"

"So far, so good," Jorge said. "Since this is early on a weekday, there should be almost no traffic". Rachel looked at Adam and concern passed between them. Something was up with Jorge but neither of the siblings could figure out what.

The views of the rolling hills along the road opened onto vineyards established by Russian immigrants nearly a century earlier, stretching to the horizon in one spot.

The Garza Winery on the road to Mexicali. Author photo

Half an hour out of Ensenada, well before Tecate, an ancient pickup truck pulled up behind the rig. Jorge signaled the pickup to pass as he could see far enough ahead to know it was safe.

Just as the pickup came alongside, Adam saw the gleam of sunlight on the barrel of a .30-06 rifle stuck out the window. There were three men dressed in black wearing black full head masks in the truck. The gun was pointed at Jorge. Mr. Fuller's gun collection included a well-cared-for .30-06 that Adam and Rachel had both used on a firing range. There wasn't much doubt in Adam's mind that a bullet from that gun would hurt. Jorge said, "Uh, oh, they want us to stop."

Rachel shouted, "Run them off the road!"

Jorge responded, "I can't risk a bullet through the side of the cab that kills you!" He began to slow down looking for a place to pull over.

Without saying anything, Adam reached under the dash and activated the emergency beacon, sending the distress signal to Montenegro's office in Ensenada. Montenegro would know where the truck was and the time of the alert and be able to direct the police to exactly where they were. Adam never expected to use the emergency signal so soon.

Jorge's eyes widened and he shouted, "What did you just do?"

"I saw something loose under the dash. Jorge, let's try to outrun them after they stop and block them from passing us."

Jorge hesitated then said, "They think we're carrying cash, but we're not. They'll let us go." Adam thought: he didn't address my point.

The rig slowed to a halt as the pickup truck pulled in front to block the tractor trailer from moving forward. Two of the men jumped out, both armed. The third man remained at the wheel of the pickup.

Rachel, looking the pickup truck over, said, "Adam, that's one fast tub."

"Gotcha. Bundle of snakes exhaust system exiting ahead of the rear wheels. P-Zero tires. Bet that sucker goes. The license plate is covered, too." Adam knew the P-Zero Pirelli tires were rated for 170 MPH. This truck was a wolf in sheep's clothing.

The two masked men arrived at Jorge's side of the truck and ordered everyone out. Rachel noticed that one of the men had a skull and crossbones tattoo on his left biceps, the word 'Amor' under it. She couldn't see his other arm. They lined Jorge, Adam and Rachel up in front of the rig just off the pavement.

Jorge said, voice shaking, "What do you want?"

The man with the tattoo said, "Shut up! I'm asking the questions here. What're you carrying?" Rachel thought the speaker's voice was familiar.

"Peppers. Bound for Mexicali," Jorge responded.

"Do you have guns?" Tattoo asked.

"No!" Jorge responded. Rachel wondered where the traffic had gone. Surely someone would come by and see what was happening.

"Are you carrying cash?"

"No."

"Too bad, hombre, because now we've got to take us some hostages which is the same as cash." This came from Tattoo's accomplice who had a deep raspy voice. He motioned for Adam and Rachel to go to the pickup. Adam thought he'd heard that raspy voice before but wasn't making a connection.

Needing a delay, Adam said, "Let me see if I've got cash," as he turned back to the rig.

Raspy shouted, "NO WAY! Get in the pickup NOW!" To emphasize the point he raised the 9MM Beretta pistol he'd been brandishing and shot out the left front headlight on the new Ford tractor.

Adam and Rachel turned as one to head for the pickup. Rachel caught Adam's eye and whispered, "Check the guy with the tattoo. He's got a ponytail hidden under the mask which covers the back of his head. Bet he's the one we saw in that speed boat off South Coronado." Adam saw that Rachel was right. Again.

Jorge interjected, "Wait! Take me instead. They're just children."

Tattoo said, "But these are rich American children, my friend. We'd take you too but we don't have enough room for everyone."

Just then the Italian air horn on the pickup sounded a mighty blast, causing Rachel to jump back from the sound. The man at the wheel shouted, "Let's get the show on the road!"

As Adam and Rachel exchanged frightened glances and headed for the pickup, the unexpected but welcome sounds of police sirens erupted. Squealing tires and racing engines accompanied the sirens coming from the direction of Mexicali. A total of four minutes had elapsed since the pickup first pulled up behind the rig. Where had the police come from? There wasn't enough time for help to come from Ensenada OR Mexicali.

Tattoo and Raspy leaped into the pickup, their hostages instantly forgotten. The scream of a supercharged V-8 engine sounded. The oversize high performance rear tires twisted into action, throwing stones at the would-be hostages. The pickup truck hurtled down the road in the direction of the oncoming sirens.

As the pickup disappeared around the next bend, two Baja licensed black police cars roared into view and slid to a stop beside the rig. Two officers jumped out of each car, guns drawn.

The first officer out said, "What's going on? We got a message a few minutes ago that you're in trouble. We're on our way into Ensenada on another matter."

Rachel spoke up. "Masked men in that pickup truck that just passed you going the other way tried to kidnap us."

The first officer spoke again. "Díaz, get them!" Two officers leaped into the second police car, spun a half donut and took off toward Mexicali the way they'd just come. The police cars were fast, too, but the pickup had a big head start.

The first officer came up to Rachel and Adam and said, "My name is Feliciano. Federal drug interdiction officer. We'll radio for help and lead you toward Mexicali until the backup unit can join us. When the backup unit takes over, we've got to split off and turn back toward Ensenada."

Adam and Rachel leaped into the rig. Jorge eased the truck forward as the police escort spun around and assumed the lead position in the two vehicle caravan.

"My heart is still going so fast I think it might burst," said Rachel, using one of her favorite expressions.

Adam said, "We owe Mr. Montenegro big time." Adam suddenly realized that Jorge was silent, watching him.

"Jorge, we still going to make this delivery?" Rachel asked to take the heat off Adam. *

"Sure, we go ahead and make the delivery, especially with the police escort. We're only an hour out of Mexicali. We'll grab some food and head back as soon as we drop this loaded trailer off and pick up an empty one to take back."

At the Chinese restaurant in Mexicali, Adam ordered two thousand pounds of Chinese soup. The Méxican waiter said, "What's that?"

Adam answered, "Won ton." Only Rachel laughed. Rachel pointed out that the waiters were indeed Méxican.

Back in the tractor hauling an empty trailer back to Ensenada, Adam looked in the rear view mirror and could see a two- motorcycle police escort just behind them. A police car rode just ahead of their truck. Montenegro had delivered on a full police escort for the return trip. The attacking pickup truck that morning had escaped.

Rachel glanced at the police and concluded, "If it's just the same with you, Adam, I think I'll pass on tomorrow's trip."

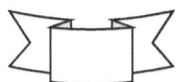

Chapter Seventeen

Headquarters

Later Wednesday, June 24

"I'm as upset as you are, Roger," said Ricardo Montenegro sitting in his office in Ensenada, a telephone in his ear. "But the police assure me Adam and Rachel will have an escort all the way into Mexicali and back to Ensenada and be here by 4 PM. I'll personally accompany the kids back to San Diego later. I'm meeting Christina for dinner in San Diego."

"At least the new truck system worked today, Ricardo. Saved a kidnapping."

"Sonia made the call to the police while I called the Chief of Police in both Ensenada and Mexicali. She's earned an early Christmas bonus, believe me Roger. Sonia's an outstanding young lady. Wants to be a police detective one day and is already enrolled at the Police Academy for classes starting in September. She believes she can help level the playing field."

"Give her my thanks, Ricardo. I appreciate you calling me so quickly. I can't believe it's only been fifteen minutes since the police arrived where the truck was stopped."

At 4 PM, Rachel and Adam walked into Mr. Montenegro's office. The police escort brought them back without incident. Jorge left to drive the truck with the empty trailer to the depot south of town.

"Rachel, Adam, thank God you're safe," Montenegro said. "I'll be escorting you to San Diego. I've talked with your Dad and he knows you're OK. I guess he didn't realize you were in Mexico today, Rachel."

"I'm in trouble there. Just wanted to see what Adam's been up to and help him if I can." Rachel looked really chagrined.

Montenegro continued, "We'll stop at the police station here in Ensenada on the way so you can give your statement about what happened."

Rachel spoke up. "Adam and I recognized one of the kidnappers. We saw him in May off South Coronado Island. He was driving a speed boat that almost ran us down."

"The police will be most interested in any information you can give them, Rachel," Montenegro said.

Sonia, back from an errand, stuck her head in the door. "I'm so glad you're safe! It's so good to see you two!"

Adam waved to Sonia, saying, "You saved our bacon, Sonia. If you hadn't moved so fast, we'd be in a bad place right now."

"Thank the police department. They had two cars within minutes of where you were. But the credit is appreciated, anyway," she said, blushing at Adam's look. Adam felt his pulse race.

Rachel followed Adam's lead. "Sonia, we know where the credit belongs," Rachel said, elbowing Adam aside and giving Sonia a hug. Since the party, they'd become good friends.

Montenegro said, "Adam, the drug sniffers that we put on the second truck yesterday also paid off with an alarm today. We were shipping tomatoes to San Diego and the second truck stopped short of the border in Tijuana – we could see that on the real time GPS data."

"What happened?" Adam responded.

"Shortly after the truck started up again, I received the electronic report here and another report came in to the truck depot. The onboard sniffers had picked up heroin. We notified the Federal and local police, the DEA, and the U.S. Customs Department. Minutes later, our truck took an off course left turn at an intersection, but the police immediately pulled it over, and escorted it to the San Ysidro crossing. At the border, the truck was pulled into secondary inspection. The drug dogs found ten bags of heroin in a box built to fit along the chassis. The onboard electronics worked, Adam. That is so cool. But someone must have warned our truck driver to make that turn away from the border. Someone inside México-American maybe intercepted the alarm at the depot, or someone in the police department tipped the drug trafficking organization. I'm betting it was in the police organization. I'm sure it was outside our company."

"Wow, good start for our electronics upgrades, Mr. Montenegro," Adam responded, pleased. "Two for two."

"The police arrested our driver for questioning, of course, who claimed he'd gotten a message from our truck depot to make an additional stop in Tijuana. So he may be clean. But that suggests that someone at our depot is working for the drug cartels and I just cannot believe that." Montenegro let out a big sigh. Then he said, "Now, we must go."

Rachel hugged Sonia again on the way out. "I'm so glad you stayed with us for the party last weekend, Sonia. Alex really likes you."

Sonia smiled. "He likes to dance, I like to dance. Maybe we can get together again in San Diego. My Mom and I like to go shopping in Fashion Valley, so I'll call the next time we head to San Diego." Rachel noticed that Adam looked pleased, but whether that was from what Mr. Montenegro said about the truck electronics program, or the thought of Sonia's long, jet black hair resting on a pillow just down the hall from his own, she couldn't tell.

"Let's do it!" Rachel said as she left.

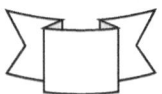

Chapter Eighteen

Repercussions

Wednesday Evening, June 24

"Rachel, we can't believe you pulled that stunt. One day off the end of your last grounding. Bad enough for Adam to come so close to being kidnapped, but you weren't even supposed to be in México. You're so grounded again. Twice this summer! This is what you'll do. Come directly home after summer school every day, no parties, no cell phone privileges. We can't believe you never even mentioned going to México." Mr. Fuller was leaning forward from his seat on the living room sofa, his forehead wrinkled in distress.

"Dad, I am SO sorry. Adam and I are on to something big at México-American. I wanted to be there myself to talk with employees, see the way the business is run. The first trucks have Adam's systems installed on them and they've scored twice already. I just know I can help Adam figure out what's going on there."

"Dad, I asked Rachel to help me look at things," Adam interjected. This wasn't exactly true but he had to help Rachel out of this jam. This one was serious.

"Adam, Ricardo Montenegro told me you're making great progress on the job when he called today. And I know that Rachel has been a huge help to you with her memory for details. But you've both got to start playing ball with us."

Mrs. Fuller joined in and said, "And Adam, don't think that either you or Rachel will go back to Ensenada before the police catch those kidnappers. They know who you are." Adam figured this would not be an easy conversation. His mother was wonderful in many ways but so predictable.

"Mom, we'll talk about it later," Adam said aloud, but continued to himself, 'when you've calmed down.' "I can help México-American with these electronic systems this summer. Now we have evidence there's an inside connection to the drug cartels at the company." Adam sounded a lot surer of his ability to handle this new threat to his job than he felt at the moment. Nearly kidnapped!

"Roger, I'm adamant. This has got to stop. We're dealing with my future grandchildren here." Mr. Fuller would expect her to say that, a favorite phrase whenever danger loomed for either Adam or Rachel.

"Mom," Rachel interjected. "Adam and I can help the police find these kidnappers. We've seen them at least twice and can now identify them by voice and by face. Adam will have an armed escort until they're caught and I'll be in San Diego. It's not like we're new to working with the police. In the past, it's always succeeded. We've never stuck our necks out."

Adam thought that she was stretching a bit here and there, but he admired the way Rachel marshaled her arguments, assumed that arch of her neck and upped the intensity and urgency in her voice. She'd been the one to recognize the raspy voice on Scarface, which had eluded Adam. He liked working with Rachel to solve crimes and she was fun to be with, too. He needed her skills.

Mr. Fuller weighed in. "I've talked with Montenegro about the safety issue. He's promised armed guards from the border south. But there is no question about both of you going together. No way! Jennifer, Ricardo is simply the best and I'm satisfied with these new security arrangements for Adam."

"Roger, you're looking at this through rose colored glasses. We'll talk about this again before any decisions are made." Mrs. Fuller paused and looked out the window. She sighed, brightened and said, "But meanwhile, I stopped by the Incredible Cheesecake Company and picked up a Bailey's Irish Cream cheesecake to celebrate your return."

Rachel knew her mother was shaky over the day's events and needed reinforcement. She ran to her, gave her a big hug, and said, "Mom, my favorite cheesecake!"

Adam couldn't remember ever enjoying his own bed as much as he did that night.

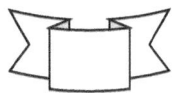

Chapter Nineteen

Second Chance

Monday, June 29

Adam met Rolando Suarez, the private detective hired by Méxican-American, outside the insurance office on the U.S. side of the border at San Ysidro at 6 AM as planned.

"Ready to go, Adam?" Rolando's greeting was warm and sincere and he reached out with a firm handshake.

Adam instantly liked his mustachioed body guard. Adam had spent four quiet days at home with the family to recover from the kidnapping attempt. He responded, "Yes, sir! Ready to roll."

The pair jumped into the Méxican-American pickup truck and headed across the border toward Ensenada. They were awarded the green inspection light and didn't have to stop for Méxican customs.

"I'm told we'll be riding the melon truck from Compañias Ferrér to Tijuana today. So let's just drive straight to Doña Inez' restaurant for breakfast first," Rolando said, grinning with anticipation.

"Good plan, Mr. Suarez. I've been there with Mr. Delgado and Mr. Ferrér for lunch and really liked the chilaquiles. Afterwards I'll need to check the truck before we leave Ferrér's. I'd appreciate your keeping an eye out for me while I do it." Rolando had been briefed on Adam's role in providing electronics on the trucks.

"OK, my friend. We'll have plenty of time to do that before the truck leaves the melon farm."

Breakfast was so Méxican. Rolando described his family of two little boys and a girl between bites of steak as Adam wolfed down the huevos rancheros with salsa and corn tortillas which Rolando recommended.

After they arrived at the farm, Adam ducked underneath the already loaded trailer with his fingerprint kit and took many samples while Rolando played lookout. The tractor was already hooked up to the trailer.

The driver hadn't yet arrived. Adam wondered who it would be. He finished his outside work and then went into the tractor cab for another few minutes. Adam completed his project and put the fingerprint kit in his duffle bag, which he stuffed under the passenger seat in the big tractor. Just then, Jorge Camarena, the driver from last week's interrupted run drove up in an old Chevy sedan. Adam got out of the truck cab.

"What are you up to there, Adam?" he said as he walked up.

Adam smiled at Jorge and said, "Good morning, Jorge, I'd like you to meet Rolando. Rolando will be going with us today." Adam deliberately ignored Jorge's question.

Jorge seemed surprised at the news about the new ride-along, but said, "I think Rachel was prettier," as he shook Rolando's hand. "Glad to have you with us." Rolando, who had only heard about Rachel's good looks, smiled in appreciation of the joke.

Jorge said, "Let me check in with the farm office, then we are underway."

Adam pulled Rolando aside. "Rolando, I've left my padlocked kit under the passenger's seat in the tractor. If anything should happen today, be sure to get that kit to Mr. Montenegro."

Rolando nodded agreement, then said, "Sure thing, Adam. No worries though, nothing is going to happen," as he patted the 9MM Beretta in the shoulder holster under his jacket. Rolando then called Sonia on his cell phone with an update on where they'd left the kit.

When Rolando finished the call he turned to Adam. "Sonia sends you best wishes and asks you to thank Rachel again for arranging that party two weeks ago. Did you have a date with Sonia, Adam?"

"Naw, I've already got a special girlfriend," Adam said, smiling. "Sonia had a date with Alex Sandusky, a family friend, but she stayed at our house as a guest of my sister's. Sonia's a cool lady, though."

"All the unmarried truck drivers in Méxican-American would've traded places with your friend Alex in a heartbeat," Rolando said. "And some of the married ones, too." He winked at Adam who guessed that second group also included Rolando.

Adam noticed through the window of the farm office that Jorge was still on the phone. When Jorge came out, Adam said, "Good morning, again. Long phone call!"

Jorge shrugged and said, "They put me on hold. But everything is OK. We can leave."

The three jumped into the tractor cab, Jorge started the engine, and they pulled slowly out onto the road to the main highway. Adam was riding in the middle.

Rolando asked, "You going to be a regular on these truck runs, Adam?"

"No, this is my last trip. We've made refinements to the electronics systems and I'm checking them out today. This should be it."

Rolando said, "And here I was hoping for a long term assignment."

After passing through Ensenada and starting north toward Tijuana on Highway 1, Adam jokingly said, "Let's not stop this time".

Jorge looked at Adam, and said, "OK with me, Adam."

Without a stop, they should be in Tijuana within an hour.

Jorge turned on Radio 94.5, a popular easy listening Méxican radio station as they proceeded to take the long climb up and out of Ensenada. Adam thought to himself that this route had to be one of the most beautiful in the world. Here the vistas of the ocean took your breath away, the vertical drop to the water in the hundreds of feet. The mountains to the east were sharply etched against the morning sky. There was virtually no traffic in either direction at this early hour. The ride was totally uneventful. No one said much.

It happened suddenly. Out of the corner of his eye, Adam saw the same battered pickup truck pull alongside. Adam nudged Rolando and pointed to their left. Jorge had already seen the pickup. There were only two masked men in the pickup this time. The Méxican-American tractor-trailer was not more than two miles south of Rosarita Beach when Jorge slowed and pulled the rig onto the shoulder of the road and to a stop.

Adam doubled himself forward in the seat then punched the emergency alert location transmitter he carried in his jacket pocket. The masked "Tattoo" leaped out of the pickup truck and unloaded four quick rounds from his AK-47 through the windshield. Rolando, already leaning out the passenger side window, got off two shots from his Beretta both hitting the pickup truck with loud metallic pinging noises. But Rolando slumped backward in the cab and Adam stayed down.

Tattoo had the passenger's door open before Adam could straighten up. He pulled Adam out of the truck over Rolando's unmoving body. Adam noticed that no cars passed them in either direction. Bad luck! Adam also noticed that Jorge was strangely silent again as Tattoo shoved Adam into the old pickup truck. The pickup truck then roared off down the road, leaving Highway 1 at the next exit for the back roads. Raspy held a smelly, wet handkerchief over

Adam's face. The last thing Adam remembered thinking was, "What an engine this thing has!" and then, "That smell is ether."

Tattoo, now the driver, chirped the tires with a downshift and slid around the turn as Adam passed out.

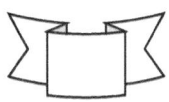

Chapter Twenty

Montenegro's Reaction

Later Monday, June 29

Ricardo Montenegro was on the telephone with the driver, Jorge Camarena, before the pickup truck disappeared into the exit from the freeway. Adam's emergency signal had worked like a charm.

Montenegro was in his office when the signal arrived so Sonia didn't have to track him down. Montenegro immediately made the call to Camarena's cell phone.

"Jorge, was it the same group?" Mr. Montenegro was upset

that he had to call Camarena. Camarena should have called him.

Montenegro realized when the signal came in that Adam had sent it via the new emergency beacon he carried in his pocket because of the tag on the message. This new beacon activated the call through the cell phone network on the Baja California microwave tower communication system, not through the truck system transmitter. Adam recommended changing this after the first kidnapping attempt. Too many individuals knew about the under-the-dash system, now just a decoy for the newer one in Adam's pocket.

"It was hard to tell, Mr. Montenegro. It happened so fast and this time bullets were flying before we were even stopped. I think it was the same pickup truck."

"Did you get a look at the man who grabbed Adam?"

"He had a mask on. I couldn't see his face."

"The helicopter for Rolando will be there in minutes."

"I'm afraid it's too late for him, Mr. Montenegro. Wait, the helicopter just came over the hill."

The chopper landed on the road as Camarena described the unfolding events to Montenegro. Two men dressed in white trousers and white short sleeved shirts jumped out of the helicopter with a stretcher. Rolando was quickly transferred to the helicopter, the new fast Blackhawk BH-60 model used by the Méxican police throughout Baja. Two of these models, flown by Méxican federal drug agents, had just been shot down by drug gangs over southern Méxican poppy fields, a first in México's escalating battle with drug gangs.

The helicopter was airborne with Rolando again within minutes of landing, on the way to the main hospital in Ensenada with an emergency room open twenty four hours a day, seven days a week.

"Jorge, wait until the Rosarita police arrive and complete their investigation. Is the truck drivable?"

"The police have arrived and yes, Mr. Montenegro, I can drive it without the windshield."

"Watch out for flying glass, Jorge. After you talk with the police, continue to Tijuana and complete the delivery. Bring the truck back to the depot in Ensenada by five o'clock at the latest. We'll have a repair team standing by to fix the damage tonight."

"Yes, Mr. Montenegro," Camarena said.

"By the way, Jorge, do you know that part of the new communication system on your truck is broken? Data on truck location is not being received. We lucked out finding you so fast." The deception on how he found out was to catch Camarena off guard, but if Camarena knew anything, it didn't work.

"No, Mr. Montenegro, I don't know anything about that. But my training on the system is scheduled for Wednesday this week. I'll be more help in the future."

"That's all, Jorge. Call me when the police have left."

"Yes, Mr. Montenegro," he said as he disconnected the phone.

"Sonia, ring Diego Sanchez," Montenegro continued. Twenty seconds passed.

"He's on the line, Mr. Montenegro."

"Diego, have you gotten to our truck?" Diego Sanchez had already been dispatched by Montenegro to secure the kit under the seat of Camarena's truck. He'd been on other business in Rosarita, a few minutes from the kidnapping.

"Yes, sir. I've introduced myself to the police and will wait until they leave to retrieve the kit. If there's trouble with Camarena for me taking the kit, I'll call. Then I'll be in your office in less than forty minutes." Montenegro was satisfied and rang off.

"Sonia, please get Mr. Guillermo Figueroa, Commander of the Federal Police, for me." The previous Baja California Federal Police Commander had been killed in January, felled by nine bullets as he waited in his car at a shopping center in Tijuana. The last shot had been from close range and entered just behind the ear. There was agreement that this had been a hit by one of the drug cartels due to the method of execution. The past Commander's aggressiveness in pursuing and arresting over twenty drug cartel members over the two years he'd been on the job was respected in law enforcement circles and despised by the cartels. The perpetrators of the killing still hadn't been caught.

Figueroa, on the job for three months now, had been a classmate of Montenegro's at SDSU. Montenegro knew that no one would react faster or more efficiently than Figueroa.

"He's on the line, Mr. Montenegro." Sonia had broken down in sobs with the news of Adam's abduction a few minutes earlier. She'd recovered and now showed a cold and efficient resolve to help in every way possible.

"Guillermo, dear friend, I need your help." They talked for two minutes.

"We're moving on it, Ricardo. Call me if the kidnappers contact you. I expect the call to come to your office rather than to Adam's parents."

"I'll be making a call to the Fuller's in the next few minutes, Guillermo, the toughest I've ever had to make." He rang off.

"Sonia, please get the president of Baja Seguros, Mr. Gustavo Rentero, for me." Baja Seguros had been Méxican-American's bank for seven years, a very successful relationship for both parties. Montenegro would be counting on the bank to help him with what was to come next.

"On the line."

"Gustavo, I hope you've been having a good day because it is going to get a little rough from here on out." Montenegro briefly explained what had happened and that he would need a large sum of money within a few hours in small denomination, unmarked bills.

"Ricardo, we can help today. I have nearly $3 million in pesos on hand and am expecting a delivery of $16 million this afternoon for a transaction this Wednesday." Combining both of these at the current exchange rate of approximately eleven to one would amount to over $1.7 million dollars on hand, a large amount for a non-payroll day. On a Friday, the amount on hand could be the equivalent of over twenty million dollars. Payroll in Baja, California was always paid in cash so banks stocked up on cash every Friday. If you were planning a bank robbery, Fridays were always better than Mondays.

Fifty minutes had passed since the beacon signal had come into headquarters from Adam's truck.

"Sonia, this is the call I hoped I would never have to make. See if Roger Fuller is in his office at San Diego State. Then track down Félix Delgado and get him to come in to my office immediately."

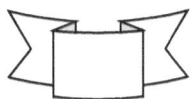

CHAPTER TWENTY ONE

FORENSICS

MONDAY AFTERNOON, JUNE 29

Around 1 PM, Diego Sanchez arrived at the SDPD with Mr. V's fingerprint kit, having driven straight from Montenegro's office in Ensenada. Montenegro waited until jurisdiction was resolved between U.S. and Méxican police departments over who got the kit. Then he gave Sanchez the green light to take it to San Diego.

Sanchez passed the kit directly to Mr. V at SDPD headquarters in downtown San Diego. Mr. Volpini, who had rushed to SDPD when he heard the kit had been recovered, said, "Let's hope Adam got some good prints," as he turned the kit directly over to Lieutenant George Sanders, SDPD officer in charge of Adam's kidnapping.

Sanders said to the group assembled in the conference room, "We were concerned about who got this kit because technically the evidence belonged to the Méxican police since it had been recovered in México."

Sanders turned to Mr. V as he said, "Since the evidence was gathered by a U. S. citizen using a private American citizen's kit, we've agreed with México to let us do the forensics here and share the results with them immediately." Mr. V was staying at SDPD until the answers were in. He fervently hoped that he would be able to contribute in some way.

Twenty minutes later, the head of SDPD forensics shared the fingerprint analysis with Jake Steinberg, Sanders and Volpini. Four sets of readable prints had been obtained, including one of Adam's. Adam's prints had been on file since Adam's earlier work in *Death by Design*. The other three sets were wired to Ensenada police for comparison with Méxican-American employee records with copies to all the Méxican police departments so they could begin checking their databases.

Volpini jumped into the police car with Steinberg and Sanders to drive from the forensics lab back to the San Ysidro police station across the border from Tijuana.

When they arrived, they joined three Méxican Federal police detectives, two Baja State policemen, and several local police officers each from Tijuana, Rosarita and Ensenada. Mr. Fuller arrived with Mrs. Fuller, Rachel, and the family lawyer, Jim Bliss. Rachel's grounding rules had been shelved due to the crisis.

As soon as they were gathered, Sanders called the meeting to order. He said, "We've just received the ransom demand for two million dollars. The call was to Montenegro's office from an untraceable cell phone. I've asked our San Diego police force psychologist, Dr. Doreen McDougal, to discuss the profile of the kidnappers. Doreen?"

A tall, red haired lady stood and addressed the group. She was well spoken and convincing. "From what we gather so far, these kidnappers are sociopaths. Human life is not meaningful to them. We must meet their ransom demands and hope to recover the money later after we get Adam back."

McDougal had earned her Ph.D. in psychology and written several books on the sociopathic personality. She'd spent over five years counseling prison inmates with the State of California Department of Corrections.

"Doreen, I know you're right. Let's get on with it," Mr. Fuller said. The Fullers knew McDougal socially so it was natural for Mr. Fuller to address her by first name. "They want the money dropped in less than an hour, south of Ensenada. We're all in favor of going ahead with that. Ricardo Montenegro will deliver the cash personally in a brief case, leaving it behind the 14 KM road marker on the road to San Quintín."

From the kidnappers' point of view, as Mr. Fuller had been briefed, this location was ideal. The road was straight in both directions for half a mile, with cross roads on both sides of the drop zone. The kidnappers had time for a warning if there was a double cross by the police. The trees there provided the kidnappers with protection for viewing the road, either remotely by video cam or by leaving an observer with a cell phone there ahead of the drop. They could watch the drop and move in by car as soon as Montenegro left, or run back through the trees to a second road and car or to an open field accessible by helicopter. The time the kidnappers set the drop point to the time they'd pick up the money was too short for the Ensenada police to set up cover in the trees.

The kidnappers were in control. One false move by the police and Adam would vanish off the face of the Earth.

Sanders spoke again. "Rachel has sketched likenesses of the kidnappers. She and Adam saw two of them on a boating run near South Coronado Island. Her sketches have been copied and are here for all of you to take with you. We should be able to make arrests from these sketches which will be in officers' hands all over Tijuana, Rosarita and Ensenada within an hour."

Mr. and Mrs. Fuller sat stunned and quiet.

Sanders spoke again. "But there will be no, repeat no arrests, until we get Adam back. Getting him back will be a special challenge because Rachel and Adam have seen these men. The kidnappers may decide that it's too great a risk to let Adam go, even after they get the cash."

"Losing the money is a risk we'll willingly take to get Adam back. One step at a time," Roger Fuller interjected. Jennifer Fuller, eyes red rimmed, unable to speak, nodded that she concurred fully. The Fullers had come up with $150,000 and Montenegro's personal bank had come up with another $150,000. With the Méxican-American bank's $1.7 million, the full ransom demand of two million dollars would be met in cash.

Detective Jake Steinberg spoke up. "Mr. and Mrs. Fuller, Rachel, we're wiring the fingerprints Adam obtained off the truck this morning to all the relevant Méxican police departments. Aside from Adam's prints, we have no match in our database for the other three sets Adam obtained. We've explained to all the Méxican police departments how we got the prints. There are no issues there."

"The fingerprints were found on the truck before it left the farm this morning?" Rachel asked.

"Yes. Some of the electronics on the truck were disabled, the part of the system that determines truck position. That's where Adam lifted the prints."

Rachel continued, "So we'll know soon who tinkered with the electronics box. That should help."

"Fortunately, Méxican-American has fingerprints for all employees," Steinberg said. "The Ensenada police will be comparing employee prints with those to see if there's a match. We've all got to head to the police station in Tijuana now because Mexico has jurisdiction on the kidnapping and ransom and is controlling from there. Rachel, you'll be asked to identify mug shots on suspects so we can try to identify the three men on the first kidnapping attempt by name. Maybe we can get two of the three this way."

The entire room emptied and headed for the cars.

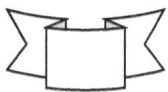

Chapter Twenty Two

Dos Hombres Bar

Monday Evening, June 29

Adam came to with a start. The duct tape across his mouth and eyes was painfully tight. Thank God, he thought, he didn't have a cold and a stuffed up nose. He wouldn't have been able to breathe. Panic momentarily set in at the thought. He breathed deeply in relief. Adam noticed disco music and the smell of cooking meat. Where was he? His head ached from the knockout drug and he was extremely nauseous. There were sounds of many people talking and moving about nearby. At least he was not in a remote farmhouse. Hope surged. At that moment Adam heard a muffled voice through a closed door.

"Manuelito, how's our guest doing?"

"I think he just woke up." That voice! Adam recognized this one inside the room as the kidnapper Tattoo. Who was outside the door?

"Good. Make sure he doesn't try anything. We'll keep the door locked. Let us know if you need anything."

"Can I give him some water?"

"Warn him that you have a gun with a silencer and that if he makes one peep you'll shoot him. Then, yes, give him some water. This should soon be over one way or the other. I think we'll have the money in less than an hour. Manuelito, turn the television up louder to mask any noise he might make."

Adam, listening, had already guessed from the TV news show that it was after 5 PM. He'd not had anything to eat or drink since breakfast early in the morning. He could sure use some water if he could hold it down. Manuelito crossed the room and turned up the television. The TV was now so loud it was hard for Adam to think.

Manuelito came over to where Adam was sitting on the floor and said, "Listen, if you want some water, I'll take the tape off your mouth. One word out of you and I'll kill you with this gun." With that, he ripped the tape off Adam's mouth. Adam had shaved that morning, but the tape still pulled whiskers out by the roots.

Adam could not prevent an "Ouch!" escaping his freed lips over that pain and immediately felt a cold steel gun barrel shoved into his ribs.

"This is the last warning. Next time you make a noise you are dead meat. The boss thinks you know too much and will probably kill you anyway. Would you like a glass of water?"

Adam could not move his hands or his feet which were bound tightly. Adam realized that he must play along with whatever this guy wanted for the time being. This Manuelito sounded like he'd pulled the trigger on that gun many times and would have no problem doing it again. Adam was sure now that Manuelito had been the one to pump the four bullets into Rolando. Adam hoped Rolando would make it.

"Yes, please," Adam mumbled as quietly as possible. With all the noise, he wondered if Manuelito had even heard him.

Adam felt a plastic cup pressed to his lips and drank greedily from the cup of water. He asked for another one and drank that, too. He had a sudden urge to vomit but held on and did not.

"If you have to use the bathroom, forget it. Too risky where we are. You should be released soon if the boss doesn't change his mind."

"What do you mean?" Adam responded.

"We're arranging to pick up two million dollars in exchange for you in about fifteen minutes. When we get the money, one plan is to drop you in a Tijuana neighborhood far from here. Where you'll be able to find a toilet and a police station. How does it feel to be worth two million?"

Adam thought for a minute then said, "Not good. My parents will be broke and I'll feel guilty. Working for Méxican-American was my idea. What're you going to do with the money? "

"My cut will not be much. Get me some girls, maybe a new car. But this conversation is over. Are you hungry? Here, open your mouth and I'll drop some peanuts in."

Adam, stomach growling, ate the peanuts. And again gagged but held it down.

A knock came on the door.

"Manuelito, we have the money. Get him ready to go. I'll bring the car around back."

"OK, boss, give me a few minutes. He's dead weight all tied up like this." Manuelito laughed out loud about his "dead weight" play on words. Adam wondered if they were telling him the truth about letting him go and whether he'd have a chance to make a break for it as he was being moved. He intended to try if the chance came. He couldn't see because of the duct tape and couldn't move his hands or feet because they were bound so tight. Escape looked like a tough assignment right now.

Manuelito lifted Adam to his feet. "Now I'm going to cut the tape around your ankles. Unless something changes, we're going to let you out in a nice neighborhood about five miles from here. Your best bet will be to make a run for it when we let you out. Before we change our minds. You're lucky. We usually just shoot 'em in the back of the head and bury 'em south of town. Less risk. Maybe our boss is getting soft. Maybe they're worried about the police being too close on this one."

"Why should I believe you won't shoot me when I start to run?" Adam said. Manuelito cut the duct tape around Adam's ankles.

"First, we have the money. Second, I'm cutting your legs free. We never do that unless we mean to cut 'em loose. Out we go, hombre."

Adam hit the door jamb on the way out, hard. Manuelito gave him a kick in the pants and Adam lurched against the wall as they went down the corridor. His legs weren't too steady after being tied up over seven hours and forced to lie in one position.

They went through another door and Adam stumbled down the single step to the sidewalk outside. Manuelito grabbed him by the arm and said, "Here's the car. Step up here." Adam could feel the strength in Manuelito's grip.

Adam stepped up to the door sill and Manuelito shoved him hard from behind. Adam sprawled across the seat where his head hit someone already in the seat. Must be an SUV, he thought, too high and big for a car.

The door shut behind him and Adam realized two men were sitting up front, one probably Manuelito, and then the one beside him. Three to one are not good odds, Adam concluded, especially with his hands tied and his eyes covered.

"Let's go, man. I want to dump the kid and head to Ensenada. Might not be any money left if we don't get there fast." Adam figured Manuelito was riding shotgun and the driver was someone new. And Manuelito had the gun, even if it wasn't a shotgun.

A cell phone rang. Manuelito said, "With pleasure boss," and hung up.

"New plan," Manuelito said. "Acevedo wants us to take this boy to Ensenada and put him on our boat."

Adam shuddered. What could that mean?

An hour later, the big SUV screeched to a near stop then turned right onto another street. Adam could smell salt water.

"We drop him here with you and go?" The driver was speaking again.

"No wait for me. I'll go with you to the Ensenada office. That's where the money is. I wouldn't miss that for anything."

The SUV stopped. The front door opened. Adam was sweating profusely. This was it. Suddenly, his door was jerked open and he was pushed out.

"Not a peep out of you, boy, or we blow you away," Manuelito said, walking beside Adam and guiding him toward the water.

As Adam's feet hit the dock boards, he tripped and almost fell.

"Watch your step or I'll dump you in the water right here."

Two men walked up to Tattoo and grabbed Adam under the arms and around the legs and carried him quickly down the dock. Adam could hear Tattoo walking back to the SUV.

Suddenly, Adam heard a second car rounding the turn on the approach to the dock. It was moving fast.

As Adam was tossed into the bottom of the open cockpit boat, he heard Tattoo shouting, "Look out! That's the Rodriquez gang! Go!" Tires screamed as two vehicles accelerated down the street. Gunfire erupted from both vehicles and Adam was glad he was nowhere close to the action. The shots were not meant for him, but he still felt the terror. Both vehicles disappeared out of earshot and Adam was left alone on a boat rocking at dockside with his breath coming in gasps.

The tape hurt his hands and his face around his eyes. One of the men returned with a piece of heavy rope and tied his ankles together again, then left.

Once again, silence reigned on the dock.

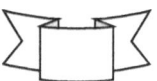

Chapter Twenty Three
Tijuana Police Station
Monday Evening, June 29

Rachel said, "But what if Adam is right here in Tijuana. This is where the search should begin."

The Tijuana police force detective in charge said, "I believe she's right. The kidnapping took place closer to Tijuana than to Ensenada. The kidnapping group has resources in both cities, for sure.

We'll look at the known hideouts in downtown Tijuana and out toward Tijuana International Airport. We have seven cars and sixteen men assigned in Tijuana and they'll check those locations out. We're working with informers in the cartels to see if they know the identity of the perpetrators. If nothing turns up here in an hour, we'll give the green light to expand the search to Rosarita and Ensenada."

The detective turned to Roger Fuller. "Roger, I respect your anguish and your wish to join the Tijuana search team. But Adam is not going to be sitting out on a street corner. This search means going into buildings with warrants we've obtained. We're dealing with very bad men. Stay here and we'll call in every half hour. This is our control center. We're set up to do this best with you and Jennifer here."

Mrs. Fuller spoke up. "Roger, let's stay here. We may be in a better position to react if a break occurs."

Reluctantly, Mr. Fuller nodded his acceptance of the plan. Just then the telephone rang and Mrs. Fuller almost jumped out of her chair.

"The call is for you, Mr. Fuller. Mr. Montenegro." This was the sixth call to Roger from Ricardo in less than eight hours.

"Roger, based on my call with the kidnappers an hour ago and their retrieval of the briefcase with the money, I believe they'll release Adam. Tonight. I also believe that this will happen in Tijuana. If I'm right, we should have him within two hours. My friend and classmate at State, Guillermo Figueroa, Commander of the Méxican Federal Police, is the best I've ever seen in México. Guillermo also made the decision not to follow the money tonight. In case of a slip up, there would be too much risk to Adam."

"My God, Ricardo, what would we have done without you?

Jennifer and I send you our heartfelt thanks."

"Let's find Adam and get him back first, Roger. By the way, my insurance company will cover most of the kidnapping ransom. We'll talk about the rest of this when we find Adam."

"Thanks, Ricardo." Mr. Fuller put the telephone down feeling better.

Chapter Twenty Four

Doubts in Tijuana

Later Monday, June 29

After a search of forty five minutes with the Tijuana police calling in their chips from their drug gang contacts, no evidence had appeared that Adam was wedged in a building anywhere in the city.

Worse, Montenegro at his office in Ensenada had received no word from the kidnappers about a release time or place. The phone had gone silent.

At the main police station in Tijuana, Mrs. Fuller sat in the visitor's office nursing a fifth coffee. Mr. Fuller was pacing the floor.

"Montenegro said he thought we'd be contacted by now," Roger fumed. He walked over to the door to the police superintendent's office. Through the glass he could see the team huddled around the conference table. He knocked once and went in.

"What's the hold up?" he asked without caring who was talking.

Steinberg stood, came around the table and put his hand on Roger's shoulder. "Roger, these kidnappings never go quite the way you expect. We believe, as Montenegro has been told, that Adam will be dropped in Tijuana, and when the gang is clear, they will call Montenegro as planned. After all, we've kept our part of the bargain."

"Look, we haven't eaten a thing since lunch. Can we get an escort to go out and get something? I think that would do Jennifer a world of good."

A Tijuana officer jumped up from the table and stepped over to Roger's spot by the door. "I know a good place. Let's go now. We should be back before anything happens. If the call comes, my boss will ring me up and we'll cut dinner short."

Roger nodded agreement to the plan, they collected Jennifer and the three went to a restaurant close by in the police car.

Little did they know then that this would turn out to be a very long night.

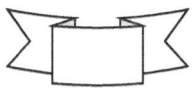

Chapter Twenty Five

Boat Ride

Late Monday, June 29 and Early Tuesday

Adam woke from a deep sleep. He knew it was dark and he was still on the boat from the boat sounds of creaking and wave slap. He was hungry. He could tell he was alone. He rolled over and sat up, every square inch of his body now in pain. Where the tape and rope constrained him, his skin had been broken and was very sensitive, particularly around his wrists, which were taped behind his back. A rag had been stuffed into his mouth.

Through dry lips and around the rag, he tried to scream a feeble "Help!" Nothing came out, nothing happened, nothing moved.

In the distance, Adam thought he heard a band playing. Still unable to see with the tape covering his eyes, he decided to crawl around to feel where he was and bumped into the upholstered bench seat at the back of the cockpit. He moved a short distance further and was jerked up short. His feet were tied to the boat. He felt around where he was for a sharp edge close enough to cut the tape on his hands.

An edge on one of the middle seat supports was smooth, but better than nothing. He wiggled around until he could move his hands behind his back along that edge.

Minutes dragged by. Adam began to wonder how much time he had before his guardians would return and see what he'd done. They didn't seem inclined to cut him much slack.

Adam couldn't tell if he was doing any good and his arm strength was draining quickly at this odd angle. Suddenly the tape which held his hands together parted. Adam immediately took the gag out of his mouth. Then he reached up and pulled at the tape around his eyes which went clear around his head. As he tugged, he could feel his hair being pulled out, but he didn't dare make a noise over the pain. A quick last jerk and the tape was off. He could see again.

What he saw didn't give him comfort. While his legs were bound with rope and tied to a boat cleat, a chain was spliced to the other end of the rope with an anchor on the end of that chain. He realized they planned to drop him overboard and drown him. At the same time, he recognized he was in the Fountain speedboat, the red color of the trim around the cockpit a dead giveaway, the same one that had almost run them down off South Coronado Island. There was no mistaking a Fountain with its wrap around windscreen, four bolstered individual seats and rear bench seat in the cockpit, carbon fiber instrument panel and helm to the right of the companionway steps.

Suddenly, he heard voices coming down the dock. Feverishly, he set about getting the knots out of the rope around his leg.

Adam didn't make it.

Two men vaulted onto the boat. "Well, look what we have here. The boy is trying to escape. Told you we shouldn't take a dinner break, José. Acevedo will be pissed if he finds out."

"Shut your mouth, Oscar. We're OK. Rafi is at the end of the dock and no one gets around Rafi. The only other way out is to swim. This water's so polluted here he'd never make ten strokes." José glanced forward toward the darkened cabin.

"Oscar, tie the kid up again," José said as he moved forward in the cockpit and opened a large duffle bag which was sitting on the forward port seat. José pulled out an AK-47.

"Oscar, when you finish tying him up, keep this trained on him. He's shown us he's clever. Take no more chances. Shoot him if he tries anything else."

"Water," Adam croaked.

José reached into the bag and pulled out a bottle of Evian. "Give him this to drink before you tie his hands. And use the half inch rope in the corner. He won't be able to chew through that."

Adam guzzled the pint of water. As he finished, Oscar re-tied his hands.

"What's happening, Oscar?" Adam queried softly. "I thought once you got the ransom, you'd let me go in Tijuana."

"Acevedo changed his mind. You've seen too much. So instead you're going for a long swim later tonight." Oscar, his face close to Adam's, grinned.

"Any chance you've got a candy bar or something to eat? I've had only a handful of peanuts all day."

"José, we got any food aboard?"

"We will in a few minutes. I'll see we give the kid something if he keeps his mouth shut between now and then. His Last Supper. Kid, you make a peep and Oscar will put ten slugs in you before you take another breath. You got me?"

"You bet." Adam said, his voice back after being dried out by the gag for three hours. Adam's mind was racing to think of a way out of this. If he could stay alive, he had a chance.

Oscar said, "Hey, here they come." Two more men came down the dock pushing a cart. They stopped at the Fountain.

"Give them a hand," José snarled. Oscar checked the leg ropes on Adam again and jumped off the boat to greet them. Adam watched this interchange and realized that José and Oscar did not get along at all, and that Oscar resented José's orders. Maybe he could work that anger somehow.

"You got the delivery?" Oscar asked.

"Yep, and it's OK if you count it. We understand the rules," one of them said.

Twelve boxes were loaded aboard. José opened the first box. Adam could see what was being counted. Twenty one-kilo plastic bags of white cocaine powder. Twelve boxes, two hundred forty kilos - a fortune – nearly ten million dollars if Mr. V was right about the street price. Two additional boxes came aboard and were set aside. These boxes Adam soon figured out from what José said were methamphetamines, also in plastic bags. Worth less but was also counted out as twenty one-kilo bags in each box. Part of the larger shipment.

José opened two bags at random and tasted the contents. Satisfied, he closed the bags again and taped them up. He turned to Oscar and said, "Wrap each box in two layers of garbage bags. Tape each layer tight. Your life depends on making them watertight, Oscar. Then put them below and forward in the cabin. We're going to need space for people."

The delivery men left and the waterfront was quiet again as Oscar finished his assignment. José kept looking toward the shore.

An hour or more went by. Adam had to guess at that since his watch was tied behind his back again.

José disappeared down the companionway into the cabin. The lights below flicked on. Adam moved around on the cockpit sole so he could see José better. He almost exclaimed out loud when he could see the cabin below.

The Fountain cabin looked like a secret palace to Adam. Purple carpeting on the cabin sole, what looked like white suede covers on the spacious sofa-like seating along each side of the cabin and an immense V-berth forward in the hull. The galley surfaces were finished in white Corian. Chrome fixtures. Everything brand new.

José was on a radio. Adam couldn't hear the conversation, but guessed that whatever was discussed wasn't good news for Adam. The lights flicked off again. A search light from another boat reflected off the radar arch above the cockpit.

José came up into the cockpit again and cleared his throat. "Oscar, the boss says we have ten tonight. They'll be here in fifteen minutes."

A man arrived on the dock followed by two women and eight men dressed in simple clothes, wearing cheap tennis shoes and each carrying small back packs. No words were spoken as they climbed up into the cockpit and were directed below by José. All the lights were still out.

José said to Oscar, "Now where are our drivers?"

Ten minutes passed. Adam almost screamed when he saw Scarface and Tattoo board the boat.

Scarface took charge. "We got fuel? You check the drugs?"

José answered, "Yes, boss, to both questions."

"Let's get going. It's already 10:30. I want to be back before two."

The twin Mercury 700 engines fired to life, pulsing with power. Oscar jumped off and released the dock lines, stern first, spring line next and finally the bow line and leaped back aboard. José sat on the second row of individual seats just behind Scarface and Tattoo in the forward seats, Scarface driving. Adam was lying behind José still tied up on the cockpit sole and in front of the rear bench seat.

Scarface cracked the throttles a very small amount and the craft powered forward and away from the dock. Oscar scrambled to pull the three fenders in and stow them. The Fountain glided out of Ensenada harbor between the red and green channel navigation lights. Oscar came back and sat beside José without speaking.

Tattoo spoke up. "I've got tacos and Corona for anyone who needs them," and opened the cooler he'd brought aboard. "Eat now because it could be rough outside tonight."

José and Oscar grabbed two tacos and a beer each. Tattoo said, "Marcelo, beer?"

"Two, Manuelito."

Oscar nudged José indicating he thought they should give Adam something to eat.

José said, "Marcelo, OK if we give the kid a taco?"

"Sure. Won't make any difference anyway." More bad news, Adam thought, confirming what he already knew. His hours on Earth were numbered. But he also got confirmation in that interchange of the real names of his two worst nightmares: Scarface was Marcelo and Tattoo was Manuelito.

Oscar took one taco, leaned around José and held the taco for Adam to eat. Adam consumed it in two large bites and asked for another, which Oscar supplied.

The Fountain was making five knots, the speed limit in Ensenada harbor. Adam noticed that despite the presence of two AK-

47s in the cockpit, and probably more he hadn't seen, Scarface and Tattoo were maintaining a low profile. No sense in looking for trouble by speeding if you didn't have to. He couldn't believe that they were taking ten human beings across the border this way, the water route, in addition to the drugs. And of course, Adam. Busy night for this crew.

Tattoo spoke up after eating. "This trip is sure easier than it used to be. The old boat wouldn't go half as fast and the motors were always giving us trouble. Last two times we finished runs with only one motor."

"Acevedo said some of our passengers are from Guatemala. At least two of them are from Sonora, our countrymen who think they can make a better life up north. Little do they know that if they stayed here and worked for us, they'd do pretty well, too." Marcelo downed his second beer.

Adam thought to himself, 'Smoking gun. If I can get out of this mess, they've just revealed who's running this operation.'

Adam sensed but couldn't see the breakwaters sliding silently past from his position on the cockpit floor. A half hour later Marcelo took the engines up a notch and the boat almost leaped out of the water. The sound through the mufflers was still quite muted.

Another twenty minutes and Marcelo put the hammer down. He hit a switch on the dash and the muffler bypass opened. You could hear this beast from a long way off, Adam thought, increasing the chances of being seen or heard by the police or the army. Hope!

The boat acceleration pressed those seated in the cockpit firmly back as it hurtled forward. In Adam's case, he was pushed to the back wall of the cockpit under the bench seat. Soon the waves were hitting them hard but still Scarface accelerated the craft. Then the ride smoothed out a bit with only the occasional slam from a wave that the hull handled easily. The passengers still suffered violent vertical motions from time to time. There was no moon out this night. The water and the skies were very black. The Milky Way stood out like a beacon.

Tattoo leaned over in the wind and said to Scarface, "Bet that bunch down below is tossing their cookies already. They were told no food or water for twelve hours but some of them always break the rules."

Marcelo turned back and shouted to José, "You hand out the barf bags yet?" Everyone in the cockpit laughed. Except Adam who was feeling a little green around the gills. He never got seasick but he'd been weakened by a day of pounding at the hands of these buffoons, it was now cold in the cockpit, and he'd just wolfed down two greasy tacos. Not a great combination to avoid seasickness.

What Adam didn't know was that the boat had already passed west of the Coronado Islands and was more than halfway to the destination and more than twenty miles offshore. He wondered what that destination was.

Marcelo said, "Oscar, go below and see what's happening. No lights. We're not using running lights or instrument lights. Total blackout except for the radar screen." Adam could see the green glow from that screen with bogies appearing randomly ahead and to either side. "Let's not make it easy for anyone out looking for us tonight."

Oscar rose quickly from his bouncing seat and said, "On it, Marcelo." He turned out the small light on the chart table below and made sure the running lights were off.

Marcelo turned around and asked José to check on the prisoner.

José turned Adam over and checked his wrists. Adam held his breath. "Looks good, Marcelo."

"Just keep an eye on him, José," Marcelo concluded.

"On it, Marcelo," José said.

Adam breathed again after José's inspection. What José missed was that Adam had been working on Oscar's knots and just loosened one. Adam renewed his efforts.

"Hey, Boss, what's that blip on the radar screen?" Manuelito asked.

"One to our left is a cruise ship. Heading for Cabo. Saw it on the schedule when I checked. That little one ahead is a fishing boat returning from the banks. We'll pass five miles west of him." Marcelo sounded like he knew his stuff, Adam reflected.

Oscar returned from below. "Two of them have used the head, Marcelo, three are using the barf bags, but otherwise no problems."

"Good," Marcelo responded.

Soon Marcelo throttled back and turned to the right toward the coast, Adam guessed, dropping down to maybe forty five knots. The switch on the mufflers was thrown and the sound from the powerful engines dropped off drastically. With the waves behind the boat, the motion changed from banging up and down to weaving left and right, becoming much smoother in the process.

In ten minutes, lights started appearing on the coastline. Marcelo throttled back once more. In another ten minutes, the white water of the waves breaking on the beach became visible. The boat was now at idle but still moving rapidly forward.

Tattoo said, "I see the welcoming committee."

Eight men appeared on the otherwise deserted beach, waiting.

Marcelo said, "José, Oscar, bring the passengers up." The boat was now one hundred yards beyond the surf line. Marcelo turned the boat around, pointing seaward for a quick getaway.

José and Oscar disappeared below. The first two passengers came up, looking very scared and now wearing small life preservers. Tattoo stepped up, grabbed the first one by the arm and lifted him up to the side of the boat. When the man hesitated to jump, Tattoo pushed and over he went. The next man jumped without encouragement. A woman followed who was crying. But she also received Tattoo's blessing of a push and plunged overboard.

One of the men on the beach entered the surf with a long rope, the other end held by a companion on the beach. He swam through the surf and approached the first passenger from the boat.

Two more men now entered the water from the beach. Tattoo reported a flashlight signal. Marcelo responded, "José, bring those packages up."

Tattoo pushed the last two passengers into the water. The rope from the beach reached the first passenger who could now pull himself to shore. The others followed.

José reappeared with the taped, garbage bag covered boxes and quickly tossed them overboard. They floated. A pair of men from the beach swam out to retrieve the boxes and four more set up a chain to pass these packages through the surf.

The delivery complete after ten minutes, Marcelo throttled up, and the bow started plunging up and down even more as the shore receded and the boat gained speed. Three minutes later, he throttled back again. "OK, one hundred feet deep. Throw the kid over the side."

Tattoo, José and Oscar moved quickly, disconnected the anchor from the boat, grabbed Adam and threw him over the side.

As Adam hit the water, he heard the roar of 1400 horsepower from the boat motors and slipped below the waves. Adam had been supercharging his lungs and figured he had about a minute to get out of his shackles before it was all over.

The water was a warm sixty eight degrees. What that meant to Adam was that the shock of hitting the water didn't force the air out of his lungs. That would've finished Adam quickly.

Adam undid the ropes holding his wrists, took six strong swimming strokes to try to get back on the surface and came up just short of being able to catch a breath of air before the weight of the anchor pulled him under. Then he turned his attention to the rope around his ankles. But make no mistake, Adam was going down. His arm strength wasn't a match for the anchor's weight even with his strong butterfly kick to help.

Suddenly, Adam was bumped. Shark! Adam's heart rate, already high, went off the charts.

Then he was bumped again. His descent into the ocean stopped. Twenty seconds went by as two animals came up from below him pushing under either arm. Adam was being lifted to the surface!

At the sixty second mark, Adam thought his lungs would burst, but he was now being lifted rapidly upward.

His head broke the surface and he gasped two lungs full of cold, clear air. Adam's head was spinning. He looked around and saw three fins in the water. He was still supported under the arms by two animals he couldn't see. Wait! These had to be dolphins!

Adam thought about the surfer who'd been saved from a great white shark attack off the coast of Monterrey, CA a few years earlier. A pod of dolphins had surrounded his surfboard after three hits by the shark. The dolphins enabled the surfer to get to shore without further interference from the shark which had disappeared.

What was happening was unbelievable but it was happening.

The two dolphins under his arms and the three leading the way to the beach were heaven sent. The trip took fifteen minutes with the dolphins surfacing to breathe every few minutes. Every now and again one of the surface dolphins would dive and lift the anchor to the surface so that Adam was being propelled parallel to the surface. His horizontal speed increased when the anchor was lifted. How could these animals realize the situation and figure out what to do? And why?

With waves now breaking over Adam, the dolphins disappeared. The anchor went right to the bottom, slowing Adam's swimming strokes toward the sandy beach. But the water was only two feet deep when the waves ran out. Adam stood, was knocked down, and stood again. He gasped for air and his limbs were on fire from the effort of the last fifteen minutes. Then he reached down between waves and lifted the anchor, walking with it up onto the completely deserted beach.

Just beyond the water's edge, Adam fell face down in the sand and passed out cold.

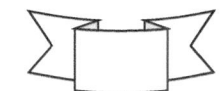

Chapter Twenty Six

Good Samaritan

Early Tuesday, June 30

The sky brightened in the east as the jogger ran along the edge of the water on the beach at Del Mar. The jogger's habit was to run before the sun rose, go home, take a shower, and meet his prayer group for breakfast at a coffee shop on west 15th Street before going to work. This was an intense start to the day, but the jogger had been doing this every workday morning for six years.

George Carlotti, the jogger, was startled to find a corpse on the beach. He stumbled and almost fell as he stopped to investigate what had happened. Then he saw the anchor wrapped around the corpse's ankles. What was this all about?

Carlotti leaned over the body and felt for a pulse on the neck. There was a pulse! Carlotti quickly turned the cold, wet form over. Adam opened his eyes.

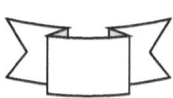

Chapter Twenty Seven
The De-Brief
Still Early Tuesday, June 30

Adam was sitting up in bed at Scripps Hospital, La Jolla. The clock stood at 9 AM. He was smiling. "So that's all there is to it."

Mrs. Fuller spoke, "Tell me about the dolphins again. I just can't believe they showed up like that. How would they know what to do?"

"Mom, they're smart. They breathe air and know we do, too. They were there when I needed them. This is why we need to pay attention to the sea and take care of the ocean homes for so many creatures. Then they'll be around for us. I'm going to do something big for the dolphins, believe me."

Mr. Fuller said, "I'm going to write a book about this, Adam."

Mr. V piped up and said, "Adam, do yourself a favor and practice your swimming skills. I've seen you lose a race to a bunch of girls at Kelsey's pool. Now I see you need a couple of over the hill dolphins just to swim half a mile in the ocean, all in the space of a few weeks. I'm revising my opinion of your swimming ability."

Adam shot back, "You forget that I wanted Julie to beat me. And this time I was carrying a thirty pound anchor wrapped around my ankles."

"Real swimmers train with two anchors, Adam," Volpini said, a twinkle in his eye showing his respect for his science student, hoping his attempt at humor would lighten the after-crisis atmosphere and move the events of the last days further into the past.

But Rachel came in to defend her brother, too, and said, "Mr. V, shall we tell everyone about the time you showed up for class with your fly open?"

Volpini gulped and deliberately looked out the window.

The nurse re-adjusted the intravenous drip on Adam's arm which was re-hydrating him with a saline solution. The nurse heard the interchange and was finding it hard not to laugh out loud at Mr. V.

She said, looking at Adam, "Let me know if you need more rum in the drip," and left the room. Mr. Fuller laughed for the first time in days.

The mood shifted. Rachel, Adam's parents, Mr. Volpini and San Diego police Detectives Steinberg and Denton knew that Adam would be OK.

"Adam," Denton said, "I hate to interrupt the story about the dolphins, but we've got just a few more questions and we're out of here. We'll have to move fast to catch the guys who did this to you."

"Fine. I feel great. Doctor says I can go home after breakfast. Be sure to put in your report that Mr. Carlotti is a saint. His timing was perfect. And I want to see Tattoo and Scarface behind bars more than you do." Adam was munching on a piece of toast. He'd already finished an omelet, a bowl of fruit and two large orange juices.

"Tell us again about the key players," Steinberg said. "I'm recording this."

"Tattoo's name is Manuelito. Scarface is called Marcelo. Their boss is Acevedo, first name Arturo." Steinberg nodded at Denton. Adam continued, "The bit about Acevedo being the boss they let slip in the truck as I passed out from the ether. They talked about it in the boat last night, too."

"And just to confirm, Adam," Steinberg interjected, "this is the Tijuana gang we're talking about, not a group in Ensenada."

"Yep. They're having a turf fight with the Rodriguez gang in Tijuana and Ensenada. They talked about that, too. After the kidnapping, they held me in Tijuana at first. Manuelito guarded me in a small back room, maybe part of a bar or restaurant. I could hear the music playing. Through the wall I heard talk about the bar and from what was said I'd guess I was somewhere on Calle Revolución."

"That helps. We'll be there in an hour," Steinberg said.

Denton said, "Rachel gave us her sketches of what Scarface and Tattoo looked like from the day you two were sailing off South Coronado. We copied them into our format and they've been distributed to the San Diego and Méxican police forces." Rachel beamed at the compliment.

Adam turned to Rachel. "Rach, I'm sure the truck driver, Jorge Camarena, is in on this somehow. He made phone calls both times before we left with the tractor trailers and looked nervous before we were cut off by that old pickup truck again going north to Tijuana. I could identify that pickup from twenty miles away if I ever see it again. Jorge didn't even say anything as they pulled me from the truck cab. How is my bodyguard, Rolando Suarez?"

"He didn't make it, Adam. He took four bullets from that submachine gun. I'm SO sorry." Rachel teared up.

"No!" Tears came to Adam's eyes, too. "Awful. I really liked him." He took a deep breath and then said to Steinberg, "Tattoo was the trigger man on Rolando. Later, in Tijuana, I was sure I was going to get it, too, while we waited to hear whether they'd retrieved the ransom money from south of Ensenada."

"Oh, God, how sad," Mrs. Fuller said. "Rolando had three little kids and a young wife. Ricardo said he's starting a trust fund to take care of the family, but how can you make up for that loss?"

Bob Denton spoke up and said, "OK, Adam, I hate to end this, but Steinberg and I have work to do."

The debriefing took half an hour. Adam finished the breakfast the cheery nurse brought. He asked if she had an extra bottle of that rum to take home, then packed up and checked out of the hospital.

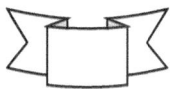

Chapter Twenty Eight
Run for the Money
Friday, July 3

By agreement of all parties, Adam's job in Ensenada was over. The trucks were up and running with the electronics packages in place. Adam was given a huge bonus from Méxican-American for finishing his job ahead of schedule and for what he'd been through earlier in the week.

The kidnappers were still at large. Adam and Rachel could do no more to help the police out on that score. Two days after being saved by the dolphins, Adam's summer was returning to normal again.

However, Rachel and Adam talked late into Thursday night after their parents had retired. Both felt the Méxican-American case was about to break wide open. Rachel broke down once, tears streaming down her face.

"What's up, Rach?" Adam asked. He put his arm around her shoulders.

She sobbed, "Oh, Adam, I'm so glad we got you back. But I was thinking, too, that I'll never see you run another cross country race, or be able to scream at you for waking me up on Sunday."

"We've got some good memories, little sister. No one can take those away from us." They talked on until 3 AM and then turned in.

Adam wouldn't return to México again but did talk with Ricardo Montenegro several times by telephone. Adam and Rachel had continued to develop their theory that insiders at Méxican-American were arranging the drug deliveries on Méxican-American trucks. The same individuals were also involved in aiding Adam's kidnappers. Mr. Montenegro still refused to believe it.

On a hunch, Adam had called and talked with Jorge Camarena on that Thursday. Camarena was defensive. He said he'd done nothing when the tractor trailer was pulled over by the armed pickup truck because he'd been afraid for his life. When Adam said that Jorge's fingerprints had been found on the disabled electronics box on the truck, Jorge said Delgado had suggested he check the truck carefully for drugs before the trip. He was doing what he'd been instructed to do. Besides, he didn't have to talk to Adam. He'd already told the police everything he knew. He hung up on Adam.

This Friday morning, Rachel drove Adam to Fashion Valley to do some shopping. Her second grounding had been suspended with Adam's kidnapping and their parents were so pleased with the help Rachel was able to give the police in getting Adam back that they cancelled the rest of her sentence.

The pair was in the family sedan. Adam encouraged Rachel to drive for practice on her learner's permit. They counted on not being stopped by the police when Rachel was driving since Adam wasn't twenty one. Their parents drove the sports cars to work this particular day as it wasn't raining. They didn't like to get those cars wet.

"Rach, let's hit Nordstrom's. I need some new deck shoes." Nordstrom's, originally a Seattle, Washington shoe store had morphed into a high end department store but still protected their roots by offering a huge shoe selection. Rachel had no problem leaping at this chance to check out new shoes. Her philosophy was that you could never have enough shoes.

"Adam, shoes first, then I need some lipstick. Finally, let's get some summer reading."

"I'll bet you're looking for history books!" Adam said, teasing.

"No, I want a copy of Stephen Hawking's new book on multiple universes, *The Grand Design*. He espouses the theory that all matter is energy strings constrained on surfaces called branes, especially P-branes. Hawking says that not all P-branes are created equal. Very funny man."

"Rach, you'll be an awesome astronomer someday if you keep at it. But I know you'd love to save the oceans, too. Maybe you could save the oceans Monday, Wednesday and Friday, and explore the stars on Tuesday, Thursday and Saturday."

Suddenly, Adam grabbed Rachel's arm. "Whoa….is that my favorite black BMW M5 to the left of us? Get that license plate!" The siblings were driving east on Interstate 8, preparing to take the exit to Route 163 North and then to Fashion Valley, the up-market shopping center.

"Don't know, Adam, this is the first time I've seen 'your black BMW'. Let's follow it!"

Adam knew that Rachel's intuitions often proved correct. Rachel moved one lane left and came in behind the BMW, two cars back, passing the Interstate 8 exit to the shopping center.

"291XR428, Frontera, BC," Rachel said, as Adam pulled a pad from the glove compartment and wrote the numbers down.

"Rach, that's the one. I got part of that number in Cuyamaca. I can't see who's driving with the darkened windows, but I'll bet its Scarface. Can you see how many are in the car?"

"No, but we're not about to take them on, Adam, no matter how many there are."

"All I want to do is see who they are and where they go. If they leave the car for a minute, I'll get a paint sample to match with the one we got from the Jag when Scarface hit us at Lake Cuyamaca. Then there'll be no doubt."

"Adam, that guy is driving too fast. We're doing eighty and losing ground. This is ticket country if the black and whites are out. You should be driving." They had just passed the exit for Interstate

805 and Rachel wondered aloud how long before either the police caught them or the BMW arrived at its destination.

"We owe Mr. V a call." Adam pulled out his cell phone. "We'll tell him what's happening. Then I'll call Steinberg."

Adam got Volpini on the second ring. "Rover to base. Adam here, Mr. V, and we're on Interstate 8 following the BMW that spilled the cocaine on the ground near Julian."

"Adam, get a police escort before you try that. If this is your drug cartel, they'll play for keeps this time. No nice boat rides on the sparkling ocean."

"Mr. V, we just want to see where these guys are going and call in the police. In fact, I'm calling Steinberg next."

"Remember, the police don't arrive in three seconds flat. Depending on where you are, it could be ten or twenty minutes before help comes if they're not busy. You could be in big trouble before they get there."

"Mr. V, thanks for the heads up. Rach, you got anything else for Mr. V?"

"Tell him you want to drive that Corvette before your ninetieth birthday."

"I heard that, Rachel," Volpini roared through the phone.

"Actually," Adam continued, "I have two questions about your car, Mr. V. If the brakes still work after I helped you restore them, will you get me an auto mechanic's certificate from the State of California? And two, if the engine is back in the car can I come over this weekend to drive it?"

Before Mr. V could answer, Adam shouted, "Rachel, they're getting off on Fairmount Avenue."

"Got to call you back, Mr. V. We're exiting at Fairmount Avenue," Adam said as he hung up.

The pair left the freeway with three cars now separating them from the BMW. "Rach, we're too far back. One stop light and we could lose them. These stop lights are so long now." But one of cars turned right onto Route 15 North, leaving them just two cars back. The BMW turned left at the Fairmount Avenue light, going under the freeway. All the cars ahead of them turned left too and proceeded north along the surface streets of Grantville.

"Bet they're headed for Mission Trails Regional Park, Adam." The kids had spent many a family outing in Mission Trails Park. The park has eighteen well maintained trails with elevation changes up to eleven hundred and fifty feet, including a spectacular 2.2 mile hike up Cowle's (pronounced "Cole's") Mountain from nearby Mesa Road. Cowle's mountain is high enough that a fighter plane hit it in fog a few years back, but low enough so that joggers ran the whole way up and back down, non-stop.

"Uh, oh, the other two cars have turned off. Now it's just us and them."

"This is great, Rach. This whole adventure boils down to a car chase. Fall back further. Easy to do considering we're still going fifty in thirty mile an hour zone."

Another car pulled out in front of the sleuths, going slowly. Too slowly. The BMW was getting away.

"Looks like a double yellow line pass is needed."

"Adam, that's lame. Don't even think about it."

"Sorry, Rach, it's got to be done. Go now." Rachel obediently mashed the throttle, executing the maneuver and returning to position behind the rapidly disappearing black car.

Rachel heaved a sigh of relief. No black and whites had seen her violation. The tension eased for a minute, so Rachel said, "How are you ever going to hold still for something as boring as building ice statues at Winter Carnival after what we've been through together?" There was a catch in Rachel's voice. The siblings had helped each other solve many crimes during their high school years, but they'd also had a lot of fun doing other things, like sailing and talking late into the night. Teasing Adam about girls or his Playboy collection was good entertainment for Rachel. Sharing the Alfa Romeo Spyder the 'rents had sprung for his senior year couldn't be beat. But she would no longer help him find his lost glasses or wallet which disappeared all the time or hit him with a pillow when she felt like it.

"Rach, all I can say is you'll have to come visit me at Dartmouth and bring a crime to solve." Rachel knew Adam liked Dartmouth College for the intense change of seasons in New Hampshire, the academic reputation, the Greek system and Adam's favorite outdoor activity, downhill skiing. Winter Carnival, especially the new Polar Bear Swim tradition, the Baker Tower chimes and the science buildings were draws for Adam. But it was hard to get to from San Diego.

"Thanks for the invitation. Adam, look out!" Ahead, the BMW had disappeared. "We've lost him. How did he do that?"

"Well, part of the reason is the road bends right there. The other part is he's turned off and it could be any one of at least three cross streets. What's your guess?"

"He's merged onto Mission Gorge Road and is continuing to the Park. I'll bet you a Krispy-Kreme run on it!"

Sure enough they spotted the quarry ahead as traffic thinned. The trip the rest of the way to Mission Trails Park took just minutes. The BMW exited left into the visitor parking lot. Cautiously, Rachel followed. The two-section, sand covered parking lot was half full, making it easier to proceed unobserved, if anyone cared to watch. The BMW looped around, stopping in the second lot.

"You win the donuts, Rach."

Rachel parked halfway down the second lot, well away from the BMW.

"Adam, it's Scarface!" Rachel whispered, as if anyone could hear with the car windows up. She knew his name was Marcelo, but preferred Scarface. The man Adam was now seeing for the third time without a mask on was getting out of the black car.

As the other door of the black car opened, Adam exclaimed, "And that's Tattoo!" They'd probably never call him Manuelito.

Sure enough, the tall blonde man with the ponytail and tattoos stood up and followed Scarface across the lot. They disappeared onto the hiking trail.

"Rach, I'm going to get a paint sample from that car. Stay here. Call the police as soon as I see what they're up to and give you a signal." It took a while for Rachel to get the signal to call.

Adam walked quickly across the lot. Taking out his Swiss Army knife, he scraped paint off the back plastic bumper of the black car, putting it into a Ziploc bag, checking the license plate again to be sure. He put the bag into his pocket.

Seconds later, back in the family sedan, Adam said, "Wow, we've got the proof that this is the car that hit us in Cuyamaca. Should be able to get them for hit and run, if nothing else, but probably for cocaine possession, too. Rach, I'm following them to see what's going on."

"I'm with you, Adam, you might need help. I'll bring the field glasses." The Fullers kept a set of 10X50 binoculars in the car. Rachel had once spotted two road runner birds near Borrego Springs using 10X50s as the pair attacked and killed a small black snake. She turned the glasses over to Mr. Fuller before one of the birds ate the snake. She couldn't stomach watching that part. Dissecting a snake or a frog in a lab was one thing, Rachel believed, but watching one being eaten alive was another matter altogether.

Adam and Rachel walked quickly across the parking lot, past the Visitor's Lodge, and onto the 1.4 mile Visitor Center Loop hiking trail. Rachel noticed the sandy colored, intricate stone work on the Center, the signs pointing out important plants and animals found in the park: California gnat catcher, poison oak, western rattlesnakes, mule deer and golden eagles.

Both were breathing heavily when Adam put out his arm and stopped. "There they are and they're moving!" he exclaimed. The trail rose slightly in the direction being taken by the rapidly receding men. Further on, the trail dipped down toward an overlook.

Rachel, looking through the glasses, said, "Adam, there is

something that looks like a brief case sitting at the overlook. And no one else is in sight." She handed Adam the binoculars.

"Rach, you're right. And our pair of fine, upright citizens is apparently headed there to get it. Bulk cash delivery to México I'd bet. Wait! Remember that short cut over the hill to the overlook? We could take that and beat them by a mile to the briefcase!"

The siblings knew this park and its four major trails like the back of their hands. From the overlook, you could see Tijuana to the south, the Coronado Islands to the southwest, downtown San Diego in the foreground and the Cuyamaca Mountains to the east.

"We've got to be really careful, Adam. Bet someone is watching that briefcase to make sure it gets into the right hands. If they see us coming, they'll try to intercept us." Just then the sun went behind a dark cloud in the otherwise bright blue sky. Neither of the two men looked back once.

"I already owe you donuts. No more bets. If there's drug money involved, Rach, we'll break this drug ring wide open with the brief case as evidence. I want to get this pair more than anything else. Get back in the car, get it running, and wait as close to the trail head as you can. I'm going to make a run for the money."

Rachel raced back the way they'd come. Adam went up and over the embankment by the trail, moving as quickly as his cross country-trained legs would carry him. His journey would take him out of sight of the two men until just before the overlook. With luck, he could grab the briefcase and have a two hundred plus yard head start back along the trail before the two men reached the overlook and started to chase him back. Then he just had to outrun them.

As Adam approached the overlook, he had the feeling

something was very wrong. Committed to his course of action, though, he climbed the remaining five feet up the embankment to the overlook and grabbed the brief case. He heard a rifle shot just after a bullet ricocheted off the rock by his feet. Adam plunged down the trail again, brief case in hand. Someone else *was* watching! Without looking back Adam sprinted ahead. He noted that Scarface and Tattoo had seen him and started running toward the overlook as he grabbed the briefcase. The rifle shot had come from a different direction. A second shot from the rifle hit a nearby rock but Adam was now running flat out. Next thing Adam heard was a different kind of gunfire, probably from a 9mm Browning pistol, he thought, the kind that held nine rounds. The two men running after him were too far away for Adam to be worried about the pistol. The rifle was a different story and Adam didn't even know where the shooter was.

Now the shots from behind him seemed to be going away from him. But Adam dared not look over his shoulder. Could the two men now be shooting at the rifle-wielding third person? He hoped so, as this would assure his clean getaway. Adam was now drawing on every hour of his cross country training to run this half mile back to the Visitor's Lodge.

Adam heard a shout and glanced backward for an instant. He saw that one of the two men was closing on him: Tattoo! Scarface was stopped, looking up to the rocks above the overlook and taking careful aim with his pistol. This Tattoo dude was FAST! Adam stumbled. The briefcase was slowing him down. Lot of weight in this briefcase, he thought. When Adam looked forward again, he could see the Visitor's Lodge and wondered if the ranger on duty had heard the commotion.

Adam's lungs were about to burst as he rounded the turn into the parking lot. He saw Rachel waiting in the car, motor running. She had opened the door a crack and Adam was in the car instantly, shouting, "GO! GO!" Rachel mashed the throttle, looking like anything but a new driver on a learner's permit.

Just then, the ranger ran out of the Visitor's Center. Rachel drove right by him, through the stop sign at the end of the parking lot, right and then right again onto Mission Gorge Road, dust flying. As they disappeared around the corner onto the paved road, Adam looked back and spotted Tattoo running off the trail, right where the ranger was standing.

"My God Rach, have you called the police?"

"No. When did I have time to do that?" Adam pulled out his cell phone.

"Adam, are you alright? Sounded like a frozen paint ball war gone bad!" The phone was ringing. Rachel and Adam loved paint ball. There are lots of paint ball games played on ranges in east San Diego County. Their favorite, Capture the Flag, was played by shooting paint balls at the opposing team using pistols. One team defended the flag, the other tried to capture it without getting hit. Paint balls really stung when they hit and sprayed red paint everywhere. No way could you hide the fact you'd been hit. Goggles protected eyes, so where you were hit was no big deal. You were out of that game and ready to play the next. When paint ball rifles with scopes were added to the game, you could be hit from a hundred yards away which raised a welt right through your shirt that lasted a week. Face shields replaced goggles. Then someone tried freezing the paint balls.

"No hits, but close call, Rach. Turns out there was someone watching the briefcase. He was shooting a very high muzzle velocity rifle, maybe a Remington .257. Bullets hit the rock at my feet long before I heard the sound. A planned double cross if you ask me and I got in the middle of it. Hello?"

The police operator put Adam through to Detective Steinberg. Adam brought Steinberg up to speed. Steinberg immediately called for emergency intervention by the nearest squad car, probably at Grantville, and directed Adam to come straight to SDPD headquarters where Steinberg would meet them. Adam hung up and shouted at Rachel to proceed as directed, glanced backwards to see if pursuit had been mounted, then snapped open the brief case.

Rachel slowed down and drove within the speed limit for a change. Soon they were on Interstate 8 west then switched to Interstate 5 south.

Adam opened the brief case on his lap and the siblings gasped in unison. Adam started counting.

"I'll bet there's more than half a million dollars here, Rach. All in unmarked $20 dollar bills. This is a big time drug payoff." He fanned the bills in one of the packets of twenties, then called Mr. V and left a message.

Adam continued, "We're in hot water, Rach, until that bunch back there is in jail."

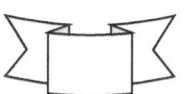

Chapter Twenty Nine
San Diego Police Station
Friday, July 3

Both Detectives Steinberg and Denton were ready and waiting when Adam and Rachel arrived.

Steinberg said, "When you called, Adam, we contacted the Grantville police and the California Highway Patrol. The police were on site at the park in less than five minutes and the CHP set an all-points bulletin on the BMW."

Rachel asked, "Was the BMW still at the park?" as Adam asked simultaneously, "How is the ranger doing?"

Denton responded, "The ranger's got quite a lump on his head. He got bopped by the guy chasing you into the parking lot before he could draw his gun. Both men jumped into the BMW and were gone before the ranger came to."

Rachel and Adam exchanged worried glances. Denton continued, "The Grantville patrol car arrived on the scene thanks to your call even before the cashier in the Visitor's Center could get to the telephone."

Steinberg picked up the story. "But the cashier saw what happened in the parking lot and the police now have three witnesses who corroborate what happened. We're showing the witnesses a mug shot of the blonde man with the ponytail, your Tattoo, to see if they can also identify him as the one who hit the park ranger. We emailed the photo out there and should know within a few minutes."

Rachel and Adam then debriefed the detectives on what they'd seen. Denton took the paint sample from Adam and retreated behind the gray door for testing.

Mr. V arrived at the SDPD in time for the wrap up thirty minutes later.

"Let me see that briefcase, Jake, I can't begin to believe there's half a million in it."

"You're right, Volpini, there's not. It's almost three quarters of a million. And Tony, Adam got a paint sample from the BMW. The paint matches the sample Adam found on the Fuller's car in Julian.

There is no doubt that these are our boys. We've got courtrocm-strength evidence for the kidnapping and now for the drugs."

Detective Steinberg then turned and said, "Adam, Rachel, what you've just done was extremely dangerous. But I want to congratulate you anyway on pulling it off. There was $700,000 in that briefcase. This is definitely drug payoff money, what we call bulk cash, and it was headed for México, no doubt. We've taken three sets of fingerprints from the briefcase that will positively identify those involved. We've had the all-points-bulletin out for some time for the arrest of Scarface and Tattoo and have just closed the southbound San Ysidro and Otay Mesa border crossings.

"Good!" Adam interjected. "I feel better."

Denton spoke up. "This is a highly risky situation for you two. When this amount of money is at stake, anything can happen, plus they know you can ID them from the kidnapping. I'm assigning two detectives to watch your home and to be with you both until we have these criminals and their bosses in hand."

Adam said, "Got any spare bullet proof vests? Our parents will go ballistic when they hear about this and we'll need the vests to protect us from them."

Rachel piped up. "You're right. For us, it was a spur of the moment thing to follow that BMW when we saw it on the freeway. Then Adam convinced me he could get to that briefcase before they could. As it turned out, it was a pretty close call. Tattoo was faster than we thought he'd be."

There was sudden silence in the police station lobby as everyone digested what had been said.

Then Rachel continued, "Wow, let me see if I can reach Mom and Dad and warn them how much trouble we've gotten everyone into. Mom is in La Jolla this morning and Dad was in class until lunch time." She stepped into the next room.

"This is moving too fast for me," Mr. V. exclaimed. "But thanks for bringing me up to date." He nodded to Steinberg and Denton who looked relieved that events had turned out so well.

Rachel came back into the room and said, "Adam, I had to leave messages for Mom and Dad. I just said we had some news to report so they wouldn't go off the deep end. You know parents." She glanced at Detective Steinberg and smiled.

Mr. V turned toward Adam and Rachel.

"You two have been awesome on this case. Too bad it took you so long to solve it, though. I'd have made a speech at Adam's graduation if you'd moved a little faster."

Rachel snapped back, "Think what a minute here, a minute there would have meant if we'd gotten through that cocaine lab quicker, Mr. V. You weren't exactly the fastest in the class with that one."

Adam raised his eyebrows and said, "A speech? In front of all those parents? You?"

"OK, OK, quits!" Mr. V said, laughing. "I've got to head out now, but I'm putting the engine back in the Corvette next weekend and I'll need help testing it if you two are available."

In unison, the pair shouted, "We're there!"

Then Adam said, "Mr. V, we still have the mystery of how the drugs are being put on the México-American trucks. But the evidence from that finger print kit you gave me points to an inside job. Jorge Camarena, the truck driver on both kidnapping tries, is being grilled by Ensenada police again today. They think he has help but are sure he's involved. Rachel and I think he is, too."

Volpini said, "Keep me posted," and left.

Detective Denton stepped out to take a phone call

"I don't know how you kids get involved in so much stuff," Steinberg said. "But I'm glad you're on our side and not theirs. Guess next fall we'll have only Rachel to rely on to help us solve crimes."

Rachel said, "That's no problem. I'm the heavy lifter on the team, anyway."

Adam came back with, "Rachel's good, all right, but she needs constant management. You'll have to assign a detective to her full time."

Rachel said, "You bet. Detective Denton is single, isn't he?"

Steinberg was laughing out loud. "OK, you two, I'll talk to your parents and Detective Denton will, too. Denton will only take the management job if your parents and the head of the San Diego police department both agree."

Steinberg continued, "We've assigned a two person team to guard your home, which your parents should be pleased about. That team should be there by now. In addition, when you leave the station, you'll be accompanied by an unmarked patrol car with two plainclothes officers. We think we're going to catch this gang soon, but you never know. By the way, recovery of drug money is rewarded and you'll both have a bit more for your college funds as a result."

Adam said, "Wow, Detective Steinberg, we hadn't even thought about it. Thanks for the heads up. Excuse me, but I promised to call Mr. Montenegro today. Is it OK if I use your phone in the next room?"

"By all means, Adam. Just leave a dollar on the table," Steinberg said, grinning. "But before you do that, I believe you should also know that we'll be having a medal ceremony soon for you both."

Adam said, "That isn't necessary, but sure would be nice. Thank you, sir." Rachel smiled brightly her appreciation for the idea of a police commendation.

Adam turned to Rachel and said, "Come on Rach, I want you to get on the phone with me."

Ricardo Montenegro picked up quickly. "Hello, Adam. Thanks for calling in. I've got news."

"Mr. Montenegro, so do we. But the reason we called is that we have a theory. Rachel's on the line with me now."

"Believe me, Adam, I'm so pleased we got you back alive and in one piece. I want to hear the details of your swim with the dolphins. Hello, Rachel. But first, what's your theory?"

"Rachel figured out that Tattoo, the fellow with the blonde ponytail, is the guy we saw three weeks ago with Scarface on a Fountain boat off South Coronado Island. I confirmed that on the boat ride Monday night."

"Who is this Scarface?"

"His real name is Marcelo. I first saw him at the Cuyamaca Restaurant in Julian just after our sailboat encounter off South Coronado Island. He scraped Dad's car with his BMW when he left the parking lot in a hurry. We saw Tattoo and Scarface again earlier today when we grabbed a brief case with seven hundred thousand dollars in it at Mission Trails Park. The San Diego crime lab made a positive ID today on the paint sample I just took from Scarface' car at Mission Trails Park. So we can definitely tie the two of them together on multiple occasions. Tattoo guarded me when I was being held in Tijuana, and both of them took me for the boat ride Monday. Tattoo's real name is Manuelito. Both of them talked about their boss, Arturo Acevedo," Adam finished, stopping for breath.

"Arturo Acevedo. I met him once. Had no idea what he did for a living. Good, Adam."

Adam said, "But the finger prints on the electronics box on your truck puts Jorge Camarena under suspicion. And knowing Jorge as I do now, I think he had inside help. Jorge's elevator doesn't quite reach the top floor, if you know what I mean. And Rachel has a hunch about who that is."

"Go ahead, Rachel."

"Mr. Montenegro, I think the person helping Jorge is someone you trust very much, who found out about the systems that Radios Impresivos put on the truck, probably overheard something said in your office, maybe a telephone call you made while he was waiting to see you, or maybe a spy somewhere."

"The police have already talked with my staff, including Sonia, but they still have very little to go on. Rachel the only ones that knew about the electronics beacon for communicating with my office were Adam, me, and Sonia. And of course, Jorge Salmón at Radios Impresivos and Salmón's driver who picked up and returned our truck. Félix Delgado had general knowledge of the truck technology you were working on, Adam, but nothing specific on the two kidnapped trucks."

Rachel said, "There's been an information leak somewhere. Which of your staff members are regular visitors to your office - who might have overheard something?"

"Félix Delgado, of course, is in here every day on multiple occasions. He runs the trucks so sees every truck almost every day. Juan Morales, our chief financial officer, has an office down the hall, separated from mine by the copy room and by Sonia's office. Juan and I talk many times during a typical day. He would have the best chance to overhear conversations. We have seven headquarters employees any of whom could also be involved."

Rachel said, "But Mr. Montenegro, my hunch is that one of them is the insider who directed both kidnapping attempts."

"Rachel, I simply cannot believe that. These employees are like my brothers and sisters. We've built this company together. Our families have known each other socially for years. They all make well above average pay for the work they do and my top people share in yearend bonuses. Last year, those bonuses averaged ten thousand dollars."

"Mr. Montenegro, Rachel is right. It's the only scenario that explains the fingerprints on the electronics box, the timing of the kidnapping attempts, and Jorge Camarena's behavior dealing with the kidnappers. Plus we now know that the drug ring and the kidnapping ring are one and the same."

"Rachel, which one of my employees do you suspect?" Mr. Montenegro said, his voice heavy with doubt.

"The insider is your operations director, Félix Delgado. He's the only one in the truck depot with the knowledge of the modifications to the trucks. He would certainly have had curiosity about what the black boxes on the trucks actually do. So he assigned a man to take them apart and find out. That man was Jorge. Delgado is also the one who had control of the daily truck schedule. He assigns the drivers to the trucks. Adam got Jorge both times."

"Rachel, getting the same driver twice could be mere coincidence. And no way is Félix behind this. Félix and I go back to my college days over sixteen years ago. He worked for my father at Méxican-American before I joined the company and would occasionally pick me up at school. We've been in business together for seven years since I took over from my father. I trust him like no other employee. I've invited him to my home many times and he's invited me to his. I'm sorry but your theory makes no sense to me."

"Mr. Montenegro, let's try something," Adam said. "Can you find out where Delgado was when the money was picked up south of Ensenada? If he has no alibi, or a very weak one, that would make it possible that he was the one who picked up the ransom money."

"OK, tell you what. Félix will be here in ten minutes for a meeting about one of our largest tomato customers. I'll ask him for his alibi for my own peace of mind. But I can tell you two that this is going to go absolutely nowhere. Even so, I appreciate you trying to figure this out. I'll get back to you later. Will you be at home tonight?"

"Affirmative. But, I owe Rachel some Krispy-Kreme donuts.

We'll be stopping on the way home today so it may take a while to get there."

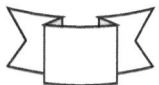

Chapter Thirty
Calle Revolución
Friday, July 3

"Manuelito, close the door." Arturo Acevedo paused then said, "Men, we let that Adam kid slip through our fingers Monday night. He can ID us and put us all in jail. Now he's even shown the nerve to steal our drug money. The ransom we got for him, of course, more than makes up for that. And we had a lucrative run Monday night, thanks to Marcelo and Manuelito, my M & Ms." Everyone in the room smiled at this reference. "All our passengers made it to shore which is good for future business and we made a killing on the drugs." Arturo nodded in their direction. Marcelo and Manuelito both smiled, pleased to be acknowledged.

Marcelo spoke up. "They closed the southbound Otay Mesa border crossing just after we went through. Jaime had the duty there and delayed just long enough."

Acevedo continued, "Good. I'll see he's taken care of. But with the drug money the kids grabbed, it's the principle that matters." Everyone sitting around the table smiled at the joke. None of these men had any principles and they all knew it.

Arturo Acevedo then said, "We'll get even, trust me. We'd have been even if Adam had gone to the bottom Monday. How did he escape?"

Marcelo said, "We think José's knots on the anchor held. Our contact in the Tijuana police department said they had a rumor some dolphins pushed the kid ashore." With that a great laugh went up around the room.

Acevedo took over again. "Our future drug delivery business depends on those Méxican-American trucks. The less heat there the better for us. In order to recover, we'll have to hide our tracks for a few months. I want Marcelo and Manuelito to go to our Sonora hideout. Send José and Oscar down there, too, Marcelo."

"Yes, Mr. Acevedo." Marcelo looked worried.

"Marcelo, did the kid see anyone else?" Acevedo said this very quietly.

"No, Mr. Acevedo, the kid couldn't see Rafi and the delivery men never got on the boat."

"Good, then. Leave right after this meeting and await instructions there. I think Félix Delgado can ride it out where he is. He has Montenegro's complete confidence."

It was quiet in the room for a minute.

Then Arturo said, "Do we have any other business?"

Acevedo's brother, Armando, the second in command, spoke for the first time, "Now explain to me how you two let the boy get the briefcase."

"We were double crossed in Mission Trails Park," Marcelo explained. "First, the kid takes a short cut to the overlook that our contact failed to mention to us and we knew nothing about. Then, when the kid grabs the brief case, a rifle shot hit the rocks by his feet. That rifle shot was meant for us if we'd picked up the briefcase!"

Arturo said, ominously, "The Julian boys need to have an attitude adjustment, Manuelito, as we discussed before. We can blame this whole thing on them. They proposed the drop site to save us a trip to the mountains again to collect. Then they double cross us, kill my M & Ms and say a third party grabbed the loot. When in fact they got it back. We should have known that something was wrong. Then these kids got mixed up in the middle of it all. Bad luck if you ask me."

The door opened and Brigantino Acevedo, the third and most senior Acevedo brother, walked in and locked the door behind him. The room fell silent. The big boss didn't show up in Tijuana often. His time was consumed running the cartel's Sonora synthetic drug manufacturing plants. "I've come all the way from México City just for this meeting. Somebody want to tell me what's happening? How we walked away from seven hundred large?" Large referred to the mafia word for "grand" or "thousand". The term was popular in certain circles in Tijuana.

Marcelo spoke again. "Boss, those Julian night crawlers pulled a fast one on us. It was just bad luck that the kids got involved. I say Julian failed to make the delivery and we go back on them. Our informer in the police department said the kids actually delivered the money to the cops today."

"Did they see you at the Park, Marcelo? Can they ID you?"

"I think they can, boss. Our guy at the Tijuana police station doesn't have access to the files yet, but when he does, we'll know exactly what evidence the kids provided and then we'll know how to handle it."

"You've handled it alright. Manhandled it might be a better way to put it. This could put you guys in jail, you know." He was looking straight at Manuelito and Marcelo.

Arturo spoke up. "We're taking action, Brigantino. Anyone the kids may have seen is going underground in Sonora until this blows over. Starting now." Marcelo and Manuelito arose from their seats as one.

Marcelo turned to Arturo, and said, "We'll get out of La Mesa if we do get caught, don't worry. We have friends there who'll arrange the breakout if this goes south on us." The Tijuana La Mesa Federal prison is the kind of place no one would want to stay for long.

"Until we know what's coming down, stay gone. No phone calls. No contact of any kind until I call you." Arturo was demonstrating to Brigantino that he was still boss.

"Señor Acevedo, we're at your service."

The meeting broke up and Marcelo, first to the door, opened it. A voice in the hall barked, "Police, you're under arrest!" Six armed officers stormed into the room.

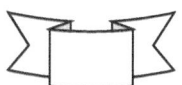

Chapter Thirty One

Checkmate

Saturday, July 4

When Adam awoke Saturday morning, he didn't know what day it was. He had the feeling that this was the day something big was going down but it wouldn't be Fourth of July fireworks. He still felt overstuffed, a result of his mother's meal of pork chops, mashed potatoes, corn on the cob and apple pie with vanilla ice cream the night before. All were his very favorites so he had seconds on every one. Thirds on the corn. Fourths on the pork chops.

Adam heard the phone ring in the kitchen.

"Adam," Mrs. Fuller yelled, "phone for you. Time to get up anyway. Detective Bob Denton. Take it here in the kitchen. I have banana pancakes ready and we'll try the Vermont maple syrup. Knock on Rachel's door on the way." Mrs. Fuller was taking vacation days from work during the stress of dealing with the police guard on her home. She could do a lot by telephone. Georgia Snitterbank could run *The Great Escape* without her. Maybe next year she would sell the business to Georgia.

Adam glanced at the clock: almost ten. Then he made his way to the kitchen, shaking himself awake, knocking on Rachel's door and trying to digest all of his mother's commands and thinking about eating those pancakes.

"Adam Fuller here."

"Adam, Detective Denton. Got some good news for you. The Ensenada police have a confession from Félix Delgado. Seems he made a slip and his fingerprints were found on the ransom briefcase in a dumpster at the business next to Méxican-American's truck depot. We haven't recovered the ransom money but we have the bank account number where he stashed it. The Ensenada police are on the way to the bank now. Ricardo Montenegro is having a hard time dealing with the idea Delgado did this, but asked me to have you call him right away. He said be sure to tell your Dad immediately about the recovery of the ransom money. I just got off the telephone with Montenegro."

"Rachel will be ecstatic. She told me it had to be Delgado. Jorge Camarena, the driver, didn't have the horsepower to engineer two kidnappings in less than a week. Rachel said it had to be an inside job. I know Camarena was part of it because of the way he looked at me. Gave me a creepy feeling."

"Camarena was booked into the Ensenada jail this morning without bail. But Adam, the best part is yet to come. Are you sitting down? Delgado fingered the drug ring accomplices in Tijuana, tying the kidnapping to the Acevedo drug cartel. The Tijuana police raided their known hangout on Revolución and arrested seven men as they left. That includes all three Acevedo brothers. Can you go with me to Tijuana police headquarters in about an hour to make a positive identification through a lineup? I'll pick you up at the house. Adam, this is the big one. We've been cooperating with the Méxican police for three years trying to get the evidence to bust this one open. We now have it, thanks to your detective work, Rachel's intuition, and some luck."

"My Dad says it's always better to be lucky if you have the choice. I'll be ready to go in an hour. OK if I bring Rachel? She needs to be there."

"Absolutely, Adam, she has to be there. I'll pick you up out front of your house then. See you shortly."

Adam hung up the phone and smiled at Mrs. Fuller. "Mom, you won't believe this, but Rachel was right. This Méxican-American mystery turns out to be an inside job, tied into a Méxican drug cartel in Tijuana. They arrested seven of the leaders in Tijuana this morning. Rach and I are going to Tijuana in an hour to make a positive ID. Bet between us we know most of 'em!"

"Congratulations, Adam, now maybe we'll get some peace and quiet around here for a change. Your pancakes are getting cold." For Mrs. Fuller, the news about solving the crime had been ho-hum compared with getting her son back from the kidnappers. But Adam noticed the gleam in her eye as she heard this news. He knew she was proud that Rachel and Adam had figured the whole thing out.

Adam bounded down the hall to Rachel's room. He had banged on the door five minutes earlier but the door was still closed.

"Rach, I am coming in," he announced, pushing open the door to her bedroom.

"Adam, what's so important that you have to come crashing into my bedroom at the crack of dawn?" Rachel was never pleased with sleep interruption, especially in the morning. And this Adam knew from experience was not a good thing. "I'm thinking I ought to break you in half," she concluded ominously.

"Rach, you were right!" Adam nearly shouted, ignoring Rachel's mood and threat. "Delgado is the brains behind the kidnappings and was getting the drugs put onto the trucks going north. He's in jail and his goose is cooked. Jorge Camarena was the guy carrying out the orders. Mr. Montenegro is still incredulous. I just got off the phone with Detective Denton."

"Wow, can you believe it? You owe me more than another round of Krispy-Kremes. A fresh donut would do me good right now." Her spirits were rising. Adam groaned and held his belly at the suggestion of more donuts. He'd eaten an even dozen when he paid Rachel off.

"Rach, Mom wants us for breakfast whether we need food or not. Banana pancakes. I've got to call Dad. He'll be relieved to hear they're already at the bank recovering the ransom money and we should get our money back today. On the Fourth of July!"

"The Tijuana police pried the bank open on the Fourth. Remember, that's not a holiday in México. Just another Saturday on the job, Adam," Rachel expostulated.

"Rach, Detective Denton wants you join us in Tijuana this morning to ID seven guys they captured in a raid on Revolución yesterday afternoon. Delgado gave the police the information that led to the arrests. Denton will be here in an hour to pick us up."

"Great, Adam, now in addition to everything else, I've got to get dressed, too." She was pleased, though, with these breakthroughs in the case. She smiled for the first time. "Adam."

"Yes?"

"I can't get dressed with you standing there."

"Gotcha".

Adam went back out to the kitchen. "Mom, is Dad at work? On the Fourth of July?"

"Good grief, yes, dear, he left at 7 AM this morning. He's getting ready for a big department meeting Monday and should be in his office until later today."

Adam punched in the number. Mr. Fuller picked up on the second ring. "Dad, Detective Denton just called and told us the case has been broken wide open." Adam filled him in on the news and got the expected warning to be careful in Tijuana despite the door to door police escort. Mr. Fuller was certainly pleased to hear about recovering the ransom, though, even if still edgy about Adam and Rachel going to México.

"We'll go out and celebrate tonight, Adam. Video arcade, then dinner." Adam loved Dave and Buster's video game emporium.

"Dad, Mom is signaling that it's time for me to eat these pancakes. See you this afternoon." He hung up and dialed Mr. Montenegro in Ensenada, getting another glare from his mother over the pancake issue.

The phone rang right through and Adam said, "Good morning, Sonia, what's up?"

"Adam, so good to hear from you. Sad news about Félix."

"How is Mr. Montenegro taking this, Sonia?"

"Bad hair day for him, Adam. You'd best talk with him, though."

"Good morning, Adam," Montenegro said, "I'm trying to come to grips with Delgado being behind this. Thinking back, when I took over as president seven years ago, maybe he wasn't as happy as he seemed to be. Maybe he thought he deserved the top job, I don't know. My Dad and I are going to the jail this afternoon to talk to him. Then maybe I'll begin to understand."

"We're sorry it worked out this way, Mr. Montenegro, but we're getting the ransom money back. I was glad to escape the kidnappers, for sure, but I felt really bad about losing all of that money of yours."

"You were our top priority, Adam. After that, yes, good to get the money back. I'll bet your father is pleased, too. I must call him."

"He was very pleased, Mr. Montenegro. I just got off the phone with him. Rachel and I are going to Tijuana this morning to see if we can identify the men who grabbed me. I'll let you know what happens."

"Adam, even though you're no longer on the payroll, you're welcome to visit us anytime. We're making good progress fitting our trucks out. Maybe you could stop over at Radios Impresivos today with Detective Denton and check up on things for me."

"Thanks, again for the bonus, Mr. Montenegro. I'll stop by Radios Impresivos if the police escort allows it."

"Adam, give Rachel my best. Eat a pancake for me. And do be careful with Detective Denton. He may try to put you on another case today. That'd be too soon!" Montenegro rang off.

Mrs. Fuller had been listening and almost shouted, "Another case? Not only is the answer to that NO, I want it made perfectly clear that you and Rachel are never out of sight of the San Diego police escort at any time today. The only reason I'm letting you go is that Detective Denton guaranteed me that all the kidnappers are behind bars."

"Gotcha, Mom." Adam expressed neither agreement nor disagreement with his mother on the issues raised, a practice he found helped immensely over the last several years.

Detective Denton was right on time. And so was Rachel. Adam and Rachel jumped into his car.

"Great pancakes, huh, Rach." Adam had eaten more than his fair share but then Rachel HAD been late to the table.

"Actually, Adam, the only reason I eat pancakes is to get more syrup. I don't drink the syrup directly from the bottle like someone else I know. No wonder you'll be as happy as a pig in mud at Dartmouth. You'll be surrounded up there with maple trees."

"Sounds like you kids have bounced right back from a tough day yesterday," Detective Denton said as they drove across the border getting the green light to pass inspection.

Minutes later, they were inside the Tijuana police station.

Denton introduced Adam and Rachel to Officer Jornada, of the Tijuana police, who explained the lineup procedure. "You'll be able to see and hear them but they cannot see or hear you. We're looking for identification only. If you recognize one or more of them, just indicate which ones by number. That's all you have to do."

Adam, Rachel, Denton and Jornada walked into the lineup room. A group of eight men were seen to be walking into position under numbers on the wall behind them on the other side of the one-way glass partition.

Adam heard Rachel gasp.

"There they are!" she cried.

"Sure are. Guess I've seen them more often than you, so no big deal for me." Adam smiled. Rachel rolled her eyes.

"Just listen to them," Denton said. "They'll be asked to state their names and occupations."

The interchange was entirely in Spanish but Adam spoke up as soon as number one said his name.

"Number one talked through the door to Manuelito at the hideout in Tijuana," Adam said. "I'd recognize his voice anywhere. I think he's the one the others call Arturo Acevedo, although I've never seen him."

The men in the lineup continued to speak as requested through number eight.

"Four and six are the two we saw in the Fountain boat off South Coronado three weeks ago," Rachel said. "Four, the one we call Tattoo, was in the truck that tried to kidnap us the first time near Ensenada."

Adam said, "Four is definitely Manuelito who we called Tattoo, and six is Scarface – you can see why – whose voice is so raspy. Six is really called Marcelo and he drove the kidnapping and drug delivery boat with humans being smuggled to Del Mar on Monday. Four is the one who plugged Rolando during the second kidnapping."

"Bingo!" said Detective Denton. "The U.S. will request extradition since so many of their crimes were committed on U.S. soil and against U.S. citizens. When we get them, these characters will be put behind bars far longer than a lifetime. After their deaths in jail we'll even keep their coffins in a cell. We'll take no chances with these killers. That number one man in the lineup is definitely Arturo Acevedo. He and his two brothers, Brigantino and Armando have been running this fifty member gang for ten years. They're in their late thirties and early forties now. Started young. Merciless to their enemies which included everyone else."

Jornada said, "Brigantino Acevedo, number seven, is the biggest catch of all. He lives in Mexico City but runs the meth and ecstasy plants for the Acevedo cartel. One of the biggest manufacturing operations in the world. Unfortunately, Mexico has become the world's largest supplier of these synthetic drugs due to proximity to the biggest customer, the U.S."

"What will happen to the factories?" Adam asked.

"They're being closed today and the employees arrested. The government now owns them. Maybe they'll become auto parts manufacturers." Jornada pumped his fist in the air. "My thanks to you both for your help. This ends a big effort for us. We'll be putting these gentlemen away for a long time. Murder, drugs, and kidnapping. Doesn't get any worse than that."

"Adam and Rachel, how would you like to stop by Radios Impresivos on the way home?" Denton said, smiling.

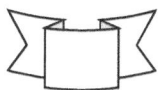

Chapter Thirty Two

Wrap-up

Saturday, July 11

Adam mashed his foot down on the throttle. The big 427 cubic inch V-8 responded by chirping the rear tires. The rear end of the car fishtailed at least a foot to the right.

"Take it easy, Adam," Mr. V. shouted. "You're an auto mechanic, not a race car driver. And this is a brand new engine."

"I had no idea the back end could get away from me that fast. This car is incredible. Sorry, Mr. V."

"That's messed up, Dude. You did have an idea and you wanted to prove it to yourself," said Mr. V, not letting Adam get away with anything. "If you'd have asked me, I'd have told you what a big Corvette can do." But Adam saw Mr. V look away as he said it, hiding a grin.

"I can't believe you got this together so fast, Mr. V."

"Well, I had some help with getting the engine back in. The rest of the work can wait a few months. Cash flow, you know. At least I can drive it now. That is, if you don't fry the engine on me."

They pulled into the driveway where Rachel was waiting for her turn at the wheel. She hadn't been worried that Mr. V would say no to letting her drive. After all, she'd had her learner's permit for nearly four weeks now.

Rachel and Volpini did a quick turn around the block without incident and pulled back into the driveway.

"Leave the car out here, Rachel. I want the neighbors to be able to see what I've been doing in my garage at night for the last three years. They were beginning to talk."

As the three walked into Mr. V's house, Adam said, "I still can't believe they ended up arresting fifty two people over the head of that investigation. Drug ring shut down, drug factory closed, kidnappers off the street. Amazing ending."

"Our *Death by Design* adventure only netted one bad guy, the murderer of the San Diego State professor. At the time, that seemed scary, but now compared to this adventure, that was a walk in the park," Rachel said.

"This one was a run in the park, Rachel. Mission Trails Park." Adam smiled.

"Mr. V, we want you at the award ceremony at police headquarters tonight," Rachel said. "We couldn't have done this without you."

"Just include me in your wills. You both keep walking the edge of disaster, I'm going to collect big and soon," Volpini shot Rachel his patented teacher's scowl.

Volpini turned to Adam and said, "Understand you're finished with the trucking job, Adam. Too hot in México for you?"

"No question about that. I was fired because I couldn't handle the heat." Adam smiled at Volpini. "But I did get a huge bonus for finishing the design for the truck electronics early. And kidding aside, I've really grown to appreciate México. The beauty, the culture, the history."

"I hear it was Christina Montenegro that really impressed you about México, Adam, and she isn't even Méxican," Mr. V averred.

"Mr. V. I'm ashamed of you. What kind of teacher are you, anyway," Adam responded.

"Your teacher, Squirt, and don't ever forget that." Adam suddenly thought Volpini was getting emotional.

Gruffly, Volpini then asked, "So, you and Rachel'll be on a family vacation in Catalina for a week, then its wheels up to Dartmouth?"

"Yep, I'm doing a freshman service project and we report early in August. Guess this is about it, Mr. V."

"We'll miss you, Adam. Well, everyone else will. Not me. You're just too much trouble for me, Adam Fuller." Adam detected Mr. V's voice cracking, so he turned away.

"Mr. V there is one more chance for you and Adam to work together," Rachel interjected. "We promised to take our good friend Sonia Vidaña out to lunch to the Hotel La Rosa just north of Ensenada, the one with the huge disappearing swimming pool that seems to merge into the ocean."

Adam piped up, "Good idea, Rach, if Sonia wears a decent bathing suit and goes for a swim there, I can promise Mr. V he'll be paid back for all the trouble I've caused."

"Adam, you're just a joker at heart, aren't you?" Mr. V said, smiling. "Maybe we can talk Mr. Montenegro into joining us as a chaperone with Sonia, Adam. I'm not sure that by myself I can stop you. And we can treat him to lunch for a change."

"Messed up Mr. V," Rachel chortled. "Let Montenegro pick up the tab." Rachel winked at Adam.

Epilogue

The Fuller's survived a fifty knot blow on their Kettenburg 43 on a mooring at Two Harbors during their Catalina vacation in August. Adam made the plane to Dartmouth on time anyway, studied science, especially courses on cetaceans (dolphins and whales) and graduated Summa Cum Laude. He went on to get his PhD in criminology at George Mason University in Washington, DC and is working in New York City at a five man detective agency, one of whom is actually a lady named Sonia Vidaña who no longer serves cookies. She's switched to serving trouble for the bad guys. The word is that Adam's firm is often hired by the NYPD, the FBI, Interpol and animal protection groups. Adam is required to travel to exotic places and is still an eligible bachelor.

He's a life member of Whales and Dolphins Conservation Society (WDCS International) (www.wdcs.org) and of Sea Shepherd Conservation Society (www.seashepherd.org) and attends their major meetings. Both of these groups aggressively defend dolphins in the wild against environmental and human encroachment. Adam has gotten to know Ric O'Barry, trainer of the most famous dolphin of all, Flipper. O'Barry is the most experienced defender of dolphins on Earth.

Adam and Julie Sanders broke up after her freshman year at Georgetown. Julie married a Princeton lawyer, has two children and lives in Memphis, Tennessee. She coaches soccer at the college level.

Rachel conspired with Mr. Volpini in solving several minor crimes while finishing high school at Seaside, like the pencil theft ring started by two sophomore fun-makers. But her heart just wasn't in it without Adam. Rachel started the Seaside Environmental Action (SEA) Club and spearheaded the Iron and Dolphin Committees. She and Mike Nelson parted ways. She never got the hankering for model trains. Rachel switched her undergraduate major to earth science and oceanography at Cornell University and now lives in Hawaii and works at a marine institute. She subscribes to *Astronomy* magazine. Rachel is completing her PhD and researching communication among dolphins. Her hope is to one day be the first human to 'talk' directly with a dolphin. She's published two papers on the subject. Rachel is dating a thirty year old fellow oceanographer.

Roger Fuller was hoping for another astronomer in the family but is pleased to have produced one career scientist and one criminologist. His fund raising for the new SDSU telescope was completed and the telescope built. Jennifer Fuller sold *The Great Escape* to Georgia Snitterbank and convinced Roger to build a second home in Palm Desert, a rondavel design. She still worries about Adam being abducted by one of the criminals he's forever tracking down and Rachel being bitten by something in the water. The Fullers found that boat trips without Adam and Rachel were not as much fun and sold the K-43 sailboat. The Alfa Romeo and Jaguar are still in the garage as an enticement for the kids to come home on holidays.

Mr. Anthony Volpini worked at Seaside well past normal retirement age, finally cashing it in after forty two years. He was as popular with the administration as with his students. Now he volunteers at Big Brother and drives his fully operational – except for the heater - 427 Corvette on weekends. Katie is still his sweetheart and acts as his personal heater in the car on cold winter days. He's an active member of the San Diego Astronomy Association, the National Corvette Owners Association, the National Corvette Restorer's Society and the Italian Cultural Center of San Diego.

Additional Information

The following notes provide more information about topics and issues raised in *Run for the Money.*

Dolphins

In *Run for the Money,* Adam is saved from drowning by a pod of dolphins. This is not as far-fetched as you might think. At 11 AM on Tuesday, August 28, 2007, twenty four year old Todd Endris was surfing at Marine State Park off Monterrey, CA. A great white shark attacked him multiple times, on one occasion cutting his leg to the bone. Suddenly, a pod of dolphins formed a protective ring around his surf board, allowing Endris to paddle ashore and get help on the beach from passersby. Endris lived to tell the tale.

In a similar documented story, Rob Howe reported that four life guards were saved from sharks in New Zealand by dolphins forming a ring around them, giving them time to swim to shore. Many such stories have been reported by sailors over the years who witnessed miraculous rescues by dolphins. Dolphins will push their own distressed young or newborns to the surface to breathe, so the behavior is common and natural.

Of the forty species of dolphins, all of which are mammals, the bottlenose is apparently the most intelligent and easiest to train. The U.S. Navy has trained fifty bottlenose dolphins through the Navy Marine Mammal Program in San Diego at an investment of one million dollars each to carry out missions on the sea floor. Using echolocation, dolphins can find sea mines so they can be removed, among other tasks. The dolphins love to participate in anything resembling a game. Recently, the Navy has started disbanding this program in favor of robots which are lower cost and more expendable.

This change also eliminates the potential for harm to these wonderful animals.

Dolphins can stay underwater for eight minutes without breathing, a tribute to their efficient use of available oxygen. They can dive to five hundred feet. Communication among dolphins is being researched in Hawaii and in other places around the world. Scientists believe they use clicks, whistles, click trains and chirps to communicate, with a short chirp actually containing many sub-signals. The females vocalize three times more than the males. No surprise there. Dolphins may also communicate by touch and through their 'dance', spiraling motion in the water conducted by multiple members of a pod. A status report on current dolphin research can be found on the National Wildlife Foundation's DVD *Dolphins*.

Preserving these creatures should become a priority.

Oceanography

Ninety eight percent of all the water on Earth is in the form of salt water and sea ice. Fresh water is only two percent of the total. Ocean water covers seventy one percent of the world's surface area. The Atlantic Ocean is growing at three cm/year due to separation of tectonic plates and upwelling of magma at the Mid-Atlantic Ridge, and the Pacific is shrinking due to the subduction of the Pacific plates under North and South America. But we know relatively little about the ocean compared with the land. Measurements by scientists have determined that reefs, fish counts, shark counts and turtle counts are declining. The causes are complex but worth unraveling and acting on, as Rachel does with the SEA Club she started at Seaside.

Mr. Anthony Volpini co-taught the oceanography course. The course focused on ocean eco-systems and pollution. Many think the pesticide problem ended when the U.S. banned DDT (dichlorodiphenyltrichloroethane) in the 1970s. DDT is a persistent pesticide that stays active in the environment with a half-life of two to fifteen years. First synthesized in 1874, DDT's deadly properties weren't discovered until 1939 when it was used with great success in the second half of World War II to control malaria and typhus among civilians and troops, and later in agriculture to kill pests. Rachel Carson's book, *The Silent Spring*, resulted in President John F. Kennedy asking her to speak to Congress in 1962.

As a result, Congress passed the act that established the Environmental Protection Agency and the EPA banned DDT. Carson pointed out that birds were heavily hit by DDT, including the bald eagle, our national bird, which was virtually eliminated in the lower forty eight states by the 1970s. The eagle has rebounded in the U.S. with the elimination of DDT. But it took years for the rest of the world to follow suit in banning DDT. The last plant in Mexico that made DDT closed in 2008, but plants continue manufacturing DDT in India, China and elsewhere.

Now we have pharmaceutical drugs which are prescribed to over one hundred fifty million Americans each year. The FDA encourages out of date drugs to be flushed down the toilet to prevent their accidental use. When you consider what two hundred million pounds of out of date drugs in the U.S. **each year** contribute to the ocean, you can see the magnitude of the problem from this source alone. This incredibly short sighted policy, which the FDA is reconsidering, is made worse when you add the residuals from within-date drugs being used by one hundred and fifty million patients and excreted into the ocean through the nation's toilet system.

Single and multi-cell cell phytoplankton blooms in the ocean cause dead zones due to oxygen depletion where fish, shrimp and most other creatures must escape to survive. Most don't. Plankton blooms come from fertilizers, especially phosphorus and nitrogen which plants like phytoplankton consume. Phosphorus and nitrogen are washed off farms into rivers and end up in the sea. This year's dead zone in the Gulf of Mexico will be the largest in Gulf history, coming from record high nitrogen and phosphorus runoff carried by the Mississippi River from mid-western farms, especially in May 2012. This effect is known as eutrophication. Sewage is also a factor. The dead zone will be an estimated 9,000 square miles, as big as Lake Erie or the State of New Jersey.

The United Nations reported in 2003 that there were one hundred and forty six dead zones worldwide, the largest nearly 27,000 square miles in the Baltic Sea, a brackish sea formed after the last ice age and bordering on many countries, principally Sweden, Finland and Poland. Another study done in 2008 said there were four hundred and six dead zones worldwide. In the U.S., there are dead zones in the Chesapeake Bay, Narragansett Bay and Long Island Sound, the Elizabeth River at Virginia Beach and off the coast of Oregon. Adam and Rachel knew about the dead zone off La Jolla, CA in 2007, very close to home, which lasted one summer.

The only creatures that thrive in a dead zone are the jellyfish. They can metabolize oxygen they carry with them when necessary. Green and leatherback turtles are the only natural predators of adult jellyfish. Dead zones are sometimes called Jellyfish Zones. Jellyfish can be large like the Arctic Lion's Mane jellyfish with tentacles over one hundred feet long, or smaller, like the black, fourteen inch diameter jellyfish that Adam and Rachel spotted near Shelter Island, San Diego, in the summer of 2010. Black jellyfish were not identified as a species until 1997, grow to three feet in diameter and may increase in number and size during ocean blooms of small organisms that lead to oxygen depletion. With the rapid decline of green and leatherback turtles (90% decline over the last twenty five years according to the Sea Turtle Restoration Project), no creatures are left to control the growing swarms of jellyfish.

In vast stretches of the open ocean, little iron is available to phytoplankton which need iron as a trace element for photosynthesis. Adding this iron to the ocean as Rachel espouses can cause phytoplankton blooms. Phytoplankton are microscopic ocean plants that breathe in carbon dioxide and exhale oxygen. Thus by blooming, they remove quantities of dissolved carbon dioxide from the ocean (or from fresh water) and prevent it from forming carbonic acid which dissolves the shells of reef organisms. Many experiments have been conducted using iron, a recent one covering an area of three hundred miles by fifty miles off the coast of Argentina in the South Atlantic in 2009.

When a phytoplankton or algae (seaweed) bloom exceeds the food supply, a die-off occurs creating a dead zone in which there is a lack of oxygen in the water for fish or other creatures in the food chain. So creating blooms to achieve goals of a healthier ocean has to be done carefully.

Small creatures in the ocean absorb the chemicals from land-based sources and are eaten by larger and larger animals. Chemical concentration is highest in the largest ocean creatures which we catch and eat for food. Methyl mercury, an organic, highly toxic form of mercury that accumulates in the body, is a good example. Some fish are so contaminated with methyl mercury that FDA guidelines limit the amount of those fish you can eat every month. The worst accumulators are long lived fish such as swordfish (thirty five years), big eye tuna (eleven years) and orange roughy (one hundred forty nine years) that are at the top of the food chain; and shell fish like lobsters. The largest source of mercury contamination in U.S. waters comes from coal fired electricity generation plants.

The information on whales and their dependence on the natural ocean food chain and especially krill is found

Effect of Oil on the Ocean

Much has been written and said about oil pollution in the ocean. Every oceanography course taught today points out that oil has had a troublesome interaction with the oceans. We've seen the pictures of dead animals, especially shore birds. Natural oozing from oil deposits has been occurring for millions of years. Man-made trouble started with large crude oil tankers hitting rocks or shorelines as well as shallow coastal oil drilling in the 1960s, continuing more recently with the first deep sea drilling operations for new oil deposits. A few of these manmade incidents are noted here:

- One hundred twenty three "blowouts" off the coast of California since the 1960s including the 1969 blowout of a Union Oil rig off Santa Barbara in which almost three million gallons of oil discharged to the environment
- Also in 1969, the Cuyahoga River caught fire in Cleveland, Ohio from petrochemicals on the water (both these first two incidents are widely perceived as giving rise to the modern environmental movement)
- 25,000 pounds of toxic drilling "muds" with heavy metals are discharged into the ocean when drilling one exploratory well (estimated one billion tons annually from all offshore drilling)
- The Exxon Valdez oil spill in Prince William Sound, Alaska on March 24, 1989 dumped at least fourteen million gallons into the ocean, the largest until the Deepwater Horizon spill noted next
- The now infamous British Petroleum Gulf of México blowout in 2010 poured two hundred million gallons of oil into the ocean, a record. Eleven men died in the explosion and fire. The disaster may cost BP forty billion dollars or more by the

time all the lawsuits and out of court settlements are resolved.

Oil companies argue that the environment rights itself eventually and life continues.

Kettenburg Boats

The Pacific Class (PC) sailboat in *Run for the Money* was designed and built by Kettenburg Boat Works (KBW), San Diego, CA. KBW got its start designing and building high powered speedboats from 1918 through the 1920's, before the start of the PC sailboat project in 1929. The sailboats built by KBW brought beautiful designs to the yachting world. Many of these designs were raced. The longevity of these wooden boats has exceeded KBW's original design goals several times over. The business continued until 1967 when it was sold to the Whittaker Corporation, maker of Columbia yachts.

KBW speed boats were twenty four feet long with 200 HP engines that would average 35 MPH in races around Shelter Island when it was an island and not a peninsula as it is today. These were popular spectator events in the 1920's and 1930's. Some of these speed boats were rumored to be used during Prohibition as rum runners. None of the KBW speedboats survive.

George Kettenburg, Jr. was in high school when George Kettenburg, Sr. founded KBW. George, Sr. provided the financing from funds received when he sold the power generation plant in New York City he built and operated. He was also chief machinist for the boat business.

George, Jr. got his start in boats by building a power boat from a kit George, Sr. purchased. This first boat was built in the Kettenburg backyard in the Pt. Loma suburb of San Diego. As a result of the kit boat, George, Jr.'s interest in boats became his passion. Paul Kettenburg, George's younger brother, was five when the kit boat was built. Paul brought his older brother tools and pieces of wood to help. George, Jr. became the designer and ran the boatyard the family started. When George passed away in 1952 from cancer at the age of 49, Paul took over KBW.

Paul Kettenburg designed the K-38 in 1949, followed by the K-40, K-41, K-43, and K-50 models, although not in that order. Paul would tell owners of K-43s that the K-43 was his personal favorite. K-43 owners accused Paul of saying that to owners of his other designs as well. But Paul did like the K-43. He took the helm of the author's K-43 for Old Boat Day in San Diego in 1996.

The first sailboats designed and built by KBW, the PCs, are sloop rigged with a mainsail and a jibsail. PC's are 31'10" long, have a narrow 6'8" beam, a twenty four hundred pound lead keel, no motor, and are usually raced with three sailors aboard. Two sailors, like Adam and Rachel, can easily handle a PC for non-spinnaker day sailing. KBW built eighty three PC's from 1928 to 1959. Forty seven, like *Seasalt* in the story, are still sailing today. An 84th PC was built by Carl Eichenlaub for his daughter, Betty Sue Sherman, when she became the first-ever woman Commodore of the San Diego Yacht Club in 2006.

James Roosevelt, son of then president Franklin D. Roosevelt, bought PC hull number 29 in 1940. He would fly in from New York, race the PC in San Diego, and fly home. Each PC still afloat has had many restorations, staving off the inevitable and continuing war of attrition with the sea. New ribs, new planking, new decks, new sails. Boat owners joke about the expression, "I think we need a new one." PC's sail well in light wind, flying across the water with the least puff of a breeze, conditions found often in waters off San Diego.

In racing, the PC competed then and to this day favorably with Nathaniel Herreshoff's famed S class design and with the Atlantic class design of W. Starling Burgess. A now famous challenge race between PCs and S class boats was held in Hawaii in 1931. The PCs won. The S class and Atlantic class boats, east coast designs, were built in about the same numbers as the PC.

Wooden boats of all kinds are still made new today. Fiberglass offers lower construction cost, easier and faster methods of new construction and repair, and lower life cycle maintenance costs. Wood still offers a better strength to weight ratio than fiberglass, and when properly varnished and maintained, gives an appearance that softens the heart of many an old sea salt.

For more information about KBW and these fabulous sailboats, see *Mains'l Haul*, Volume 41, No. 1, published by the Maritime Museum of San Diego, Winter 2005. Much of the information above was taken from this publication and from the author's personal discussions with Paul Kettenburg who owned and sailed K-43 No. 1, *Tomboy*, as well as other KBW sailboats. The author owned hull No. 17 (of nineteen built) for ten years with boat partner Gordon Knight, sailing and racing in southern California waters. No. 17 was previously owned by San Diego architect Roy Drew for twenty years and architect Frank Hope and his wife Barbara for ten years. If you like a sailboat, you keep it awhile.

Fountain Speedboats

Fountains are among the fastest boats made. Drug lords would naturally be attracted to such high performance delivery vehicles, although Fountain would prefer other forms of advertising. In addition to the Lightning 47 used by Scarface and Tattoo in this story, Fountain makes an even faster line of racing boats. More information about the Fountain boat product line can be found

Racing Fountains with the canopy configuration and twin 900 BHP engines can top 142 MPH. The Lightning 47 sports two 700 BHP V-8 Mercury engines and has a top speed of 90 MPH. This is a very nice way to go fast on the water.

Jaguar

"Making a success of a business venture – that was my original aim in life," said Sir William Lyons who started making Swallow motorcycle sidecars in 1922 with partner William Walmsley. By 1927, the company was making cars, sleek wire wheeled, cycle-fendered two-seaters based on the Austin Seven chassis.

By September 1935, Lyons was building both a sedan and a sports car called the SS 100 Jaguar, although the company was then called SS Cars Ltd. Jaguar was the model name. With over 100 BHP from its 3.5 liter engine, the SS 100 was a performance car in its day. The car was reported to be capable of 101 MPH with the 3.5 liter version of the engine installed.

Lyons changed the company name to Jaguar Cars Ltd in 1945 to avoid the negative connotations of the name 'SS' in those days right after World War II and the German Secret State police.

Then the XK-120 arrived. Introduced at the British Motor Show in fall 1948, the design of the XK-120 made a hugely favorable impact on postwar, everything-is-still-rationed England. A Jaguar XK-120 with a Plexiglas windscreen replacing the normal windshield set a two way record speed average of 132.596 MPH for a production car in Jabbeke, Belgium on May 30, 1949. Thus was the car proved to be at least as fast as the '120' in its name that implied 120 MPH and made the XK-120 the fastest production sports car in the world. This feat captured the imagination of car fans and assured the company's continuing success.

In August 1949, Lyons decided to let the XK-120 race at Silverstone, England in a one hour race but with hand-picked drivers. In Jaguar's first race, three XK-120s started (all that had then been constructed to that point) and Jaguar took first and second place. A blown tire eliminated Prince Bira's car and prevented the sweep.

To cement this performance image, Lyons was convinced by his staff to design and build a competition model, the XK-120C, a gorgeous purpose-built race car that won the Le Mans, France twenty four hour race twice (1951 and 1953) and many other road races in Europe and America.

The C-Type, as it became known, was followed by the D-Type in 1954, a much faster car with lines that are arguably even more attractive than the C-Type. Potent on the race track, the D-Type won Le Mans three years running, 1955-1957, among many other racing victories. Malcolm Sayer was born in 1916 and passed away in 1970 from a heart attack. He was a gifted design engineer who had worked in the aviation industry for the Bristol Aeroplane Company. Sir William Lyons hired him as Jaguar design chief. Sayer gets credit for the design of the C and D-Type racing cars and the later E-Type, a high water mark in production sports car design. Sayer's innovative design techniques included the use of mathematical formulas to describe design surfaces, now standard technique in computer aided design.

Meanwhile, the production sports cars were advancing from the XK-120 to the XK-140 with 160 BHP 3.4 liter engines, and finally to the XK-150, which in final form had the 3.8 liter motor with 265 BHP.

The Jaguar sedans, such as the 3.8 Mark II and the Mark VII in the early Sixties were Jaguar's bread and butter cars. They outsold the sports cars by a large margin. All Jaguars used the William Heynes/Harry Weslake-designed inline six cylinder engine of the original XK-120 through 1964 when the V-12 engined XJ-13 was produced.

Jaguar won the prestigious *Architectural Digest* award for design excellence with the new XK-E sports car in 1961. This award is usually given to especially fine buildings. The XK-E exterior design evolved from the earlier XK-120C and D-Type race cars.

The Heritage Trust Museum was created at Brown's Lane, Coventry, England, the spiritual home of Jaguar. Started in 1983, the Museum houses many Jaguar cars. The Museum was relocated in 2012 to Banbury Road, Gaydon, Warwickshire, half an hour's drive south of Coventry. Both locations are northwest of London.

The Museum collection includes an XK-E roadster like the one owned by the Fullers, as well as earlier and later cars, such as a 1939 SS-100 car, a design beauty as well as a performance sports car, the 1950 "NUB 120" XK-120 Alpine Rally winning car, the 1964 XJ-13 race car (first V-12 Jaguar), and the 1988 Lemans winning XJR-9LM, which took advantage of a more developed 750 BHP V-12, and finished first, fourth and sixteenth overall in this historically important race for Jaguar.

The classic Jaguar racing and production cars have appreciated in value. The D-Types which sold new for $9,600 in the 1950s have traded hands for over $4 million recently. A nicely restored E-Type production sports car which sold new for $6,000 in the 1960s can be purchased for as much as $175,000 today.

The museum recently housed one hundred and fourteen Jaguar, Daimler and Lanchester cars. Lanchester was acquired by Daimler in

1931, and later Daimler was acquired by Jaguar. Jaguar was owned by Ford Motor Company from 1989 through 2008 and is presently owned by Tata Motors of India. The museum is well worth the visit on your next trip to England, especially if you can include the factory tour.

Of course, today the newest Jaguars, like the F-Type sports cars, surpass the classic models in many ways. The F-Type R, spiritual successor to the E-Type, offers all-wheel drive, a supercharger, and 550 BHP from only a 305 cubic inch V-8, barely larger than the engine supplied in the E-Type.

For additional information about the cars, the company, and the individual contributors to the success of Jaguar cars, see the Jaguar Daimler Heritage Trust web site: http://www.jaguar.com/uk/jdht. Another excellent source of information is Paul Skilleter's *Jaguar, The Sporting Heritage,* from which some of the above information comes.

Corvette

Chevrolet Corvettes are one of Mr. Anthony Volpini's many passions, along with olives and sangiovese grapes. Corvettes are all-American sports cars made by General Motors. The name 'corvette' originally described a small but maneuverable French warship developed in the 1670s for coastal defense of France.

The latest Corvette automobile compares with the best production sports cars from around the world, such as Porsche, in straight line and skid pad performance. Supercars such as McLaren's, Bugatti Veyrons and Lamborghinis may go faster but cost a lot more. The first Corvette was introduced as a 1953 model, powered by Chevrolet's Blue Flame inline six cylinder motor.

Today, Corvettes are raced successfully in North America and in Europe. Corvette won the GTE Pro class at Le Mans in 2011, for example, the seventh win by Corvette Racing at Le Mans, finishing eleventh overall and beating the second place Ferrari in class by two minutes and twenty nine seconds after twenty four hours of flat out racing.

For Adam, a white car with red interior leaps to mind when someone mentions Corvette. Mr. Volpini prefers black on black, the modern "Euro" color combination. Italians prefer red, some say due to their passionate nature, but Mr. V is a maverick in many ways.

Corvette engines mark the progress of the marque. The underpowered Blue Flame six was soon replaced by Chevy's 283 cubic inch V-8 in September 1954. This engine was still the choice when the collector favorite 1957 Corvette was introduced. Although Corvettes were raced from the get-go, the 1957 model was a very successful racer in addition to being visually exciting.

Engine size grew until the 427 cubic inch V-8 arrived in 1965. This same engine appears in *Run for the Money* in Mr. V's 1967 model Corvette. This car is included in the Chevrolet design group designation 'C2', as today's Corvettes are in the Z06 group. Mr. Volpini's street version of this engine made "only" 435 BHP, while race versions made over 500 BHP. Larger engines of up to 454 cubic inches arrived later. In 2016, the supercharged Z06 makes 650 BHP off the showroom floor with a smaller engine, 378 cubic inches. The race version direct from the factory, the C7.R, is even more potent. See http://www.corvettemuseum.com for more information about older Corvettes.

Mr. V's car cost less than $5,000 when new. Today, a buyer might have to pay $100,000 or more for a nice restored example. Mr. V bought his unrestored car for a song but added sweat equity and big bucks to bring the value up to market.

Mr. Volpini's 427cubic inch/435 BHP 1967 Corvette with 4-speed transmission and optional side exhaust pipes. Corvettes have a passionate following on both road and track

Corvettes are the handiwork of a General Motors team inspired and led by Zora Arkus-Duntov, the GM engineer known as the father of the Corvette. Arkus-Duntov had his hand on many of the high performance General Motors products from 1950's through 1970's. He understood the term "performance sports car" when assigned the engineering responsibilities for the Corvette in time to bring the first model to market in 1953. He'd raced English Allards in the Le Mans twenty four hour race by that time.

Later, Arkus-Duntov introduced the new four speed manual transmission with the 1957 model Corvette followed by the split rear window Stingray coupe in 1963 and as mentioned the 427 cubic inch motor in 1965. On Duntov's death in 1996, George Will, the newspaper columnist and author said, "If you do not mourn his passing, you are not a good American."

Drugs

The natural sources for the main drug in this story, cocaine, have been around for a long time. As Detective Steinberg says, making cocaine starts with the *Erythroxylon coca* leaf which has been chewed by South American natives for five thousand years or more and was used in the 1200s to 1500s CE by the Incas. Chewing a coca leaf calms the stomach, brightens the mood and reduces anxiety after a day's work. Coca leaf tea is especially pleasant late in the day and is popular in Peru today.

Coca-Cola, patented by Atlanta chemist John Pemberton in May 1886, is a soft drink that contained small quantities of extract from the cola leaf and from the kola nut in the early days; hence the name that still carries the largest soft drink company in the world. All traces of coca leaf narcotics were removed by the 1920s. (Wikipedia) At the time there were many popular patent medicines which contained cocaine and many addicts who liked taking them, like Sigmund Freud, the famous psychiatrist. The U.S. Congress banned the use of cocaine in all products, including patent medicines, through the Harrison Narcotics Tax Act of 1914 by making a doctor's prescription necessary to buy anything with cocaine in it. Later, the Jones-Miller Act of 1922 restricted cocaine manufacturers as well.

Park, Davies, the drug company, introduced coca-cigars in 1886 but the product failed because heat degraded the cocaine hydrochloride used in the cigars, the same white crystalline powder that Adam discovered in the Cuyamaca Restaurant parking lot near Julian, CA. Nearly one hundred years later, freebase or crack cocaine solved the heat problem and is now successfully smoked for the most intense cocaine high.

Since the effect of using cocaine is short lived but addictive, the user quickly crashes and needs another fix. This makes cocaine the perfect drug for the producers. One order is quickly followed by the next. This and additional information can be found at: **http://cocaine.org/process.html**

There is a global cocaine supply chain shift underway today. The world's supply of coca leaf comes from the Andean mountain regions of Peru, Columbia and Bolivia. The most potent leaves grow in the 1700 to 6500 foot high range of the mountains. However, now the fastest growing coca leaf plantations are in Peru's remote Amazon basin, an area that was previously felt to lack the environmental requirements for growing the coca plant, let alone the roads to get there. Research has shown that the acidity of the soil is more important than the elevation.

Shipments are up seventy percent per year over the last few years.

Legalize Drugs

The drug wars in México come from opportunities to make money by manufacturing and/or transporting illegal drugs such as methamphetamine, ecstasy, cocaine, heroin and marijuana to market in the U.S. Latin American countries believe that the U.S. should curb the demand. In the U.S., blame is heaped on the suppliers.

One argument gaining traction in the U.S. is that drugs should be legalized and dealt with in a manner similar to alcohol. Prices would plummet and the incentive to fight over illegal distribution channels would be over. California has made marijuana legal for medical purposes. Several states have made marijuana legal for any purpose. The Federal government still classifies marijuana as illegal for any purpose. That legal conflict must be resolved as well as the larger arguments about whether to make the more deadly drugs legal as well.

Crack cocaine, which gives a quicker and more intense high than powdered cocaine, presents problems as a 'legalized' drug for the user and for the enforcers of the new rules. What is the allowable limit to be able to drive a motor vehicle? How do you test for that limit? How do you deal with the resulting addiction? The way we deal with alcoholism? There would be many such decisions to be made.

Prescription painkiller drugs alone kill 15,000 of us a year, more U.S. citizens than die from heroin and cocaine combined.[1] What's the difference? Laws must be enacted in the future to prevent newly 'legalized' illegal drugs such as cocaine from being abused and hurting innocent bystanders, as is the case today with alcohol and prescription drugs such as OxyContin. These new laws will be broken as are those we have on the books today for operating a motor vehicle with blood alcohol exceeding the allowable limit; or when taking 'legal' painkillers like OxyContin without a prescription. The Drug Enforcement Administration in the U.S. is continually cracking down on illegal uses of legal prescription drugs.

I believe that México in particular would appreciate the U.S. moving to legalize today's troublesome illegal drugs. Their war to control drug cartels would end. The overwhelming death sprees underway today between cartels and between cartels and the authorities would become a memory. México's resources could be more productively applied to other areas of their economy and the U.S. could spend less time guarding our common border.

Then again, it may just be more complicated than this. Drug cartels might switch to kidnapping and extortion, murdering mayors of small towns in México and snooping college students who don't play ball.

And cartels might start exporting this new business model to the U.S. The cartels may be tough to eradicate even if drugs are legalized at some point in the future. The issue should certainly be debated, however. Prohibition of alcohol certainly never worked.

---

[1] *Sage Advice on Pharmaceuticals*, 2013, Bud Suiter, and the U.S. Centers for Disease Control, 2010.
Additional Information

www.ingramcontent.com/pod-product-compliance
Lightning Source LLC
Chambersburg PA
CBHW030115180626
46812CB00002B/431